ELITE PROTECTION

GUARDIAN ELITE, BOOK 4

KALYN COOPER

ELITE Protection

KaLyn Cooper

Cover Artist: Syneca Featherstone

Editors: Marci Boudreaux Clark & Linda Clarkson

Published 2022

ISBN–13: 978-1-970145-32-8

LETTER TO READERS

Thank you so much for purchasing *ELITE Protection*! I hope you enjoy the book and will consider other books by KaLyn Cooper. There's a complete list with links at the end.

ELITE Protection was originally published as *Snow SEAL* but has been deeply edited and rewritten to become part of the newly revised and rebranded **Guardian ELITE series.** Several of the original secondary characters have been renamed or removed per agreement with Elle James, Twisted Page Press, the original publisher.

ELITE Protection is the fourth book in the Guardian Elite series, a spinoff of KaLyn Cooper's **Black Swan Series.** Although every book is a standalone, you may wish to read the books in that series to get to know

Alex Wolf and Katlin Callahan. You may also enjoy the other novellas in the **Guardian Elite series.**

Thank you for reading my books. If you have enjoyed *ELITE Protection*, please consider telling others what you like best about it in a review on your favorite retailer.

You may also want to read my other books. For an entire list of my books and details about each, please go to my website at www.KaLynCooper.com

Always,
    KaLyn

DEDICATION

I dedicate this book to the women warriors of the YPJ, part of the Syrian Army's People's Protection Unit. Keep up the good work!

ACKNOWLEDGMENTS

As always, I couldn't publish a book without the wonderful editing of Marci Clark and the awesome cover by Syneca Featherstone.

Thank you to my wonderful readers Judy Slater, Kevin Luke, Julie Kahler, Mary Brannian, Sara Conger, Diana Tidlund, and Rhonda Gothier for helping me name characters. A special thank you to Teresa Christianson, my Beta reader and the woman who keeps my characters organized. Last, I am so thankful for my wonderful husband who helps with the military details and plot points.

ABOUT THIS BOOK

Terrorists want her...but so does he. The only thing that matters is the Guardian Security Atlanta Center expects him to keep his assignment alive.

Isaac Snow believes he'll be protecting the pampered daughter of two Atlanta physicians when he arrives in Big Sky, Montana. He expects to be forced to ski the novice slopes all day and spend his nights fending off unwanted pursuers.

Hannah Kader was an officer in the all-female YPG Battalion in the Syrian Army, personally responsible for the deaths of hundreds of terrorists. The newly reorganized Islamic State wants her, preferably alive.

The chase isn't the only thing that heats up when the flint of the former SEAL strikes against the steel of the woman warrior.

ELITE Protection, book #4 in the **Guardian Elite**

series, is a heart-pounding, military romance inter-woven with sizzling passion.

Buy this book and let KaLyn Cooper take you on a thrill ride through the Montana mountains.

*Note: This book was previously published as Snow SEAL. It has been deeply edited and expanded to become part of KaLyn Cooper's rebranded **Guardian ELITE series**.*

CHAPTER 1

ISAAC SNOW SHIFTED HIS WEIGHT SO THE TAILS OF HIS skis were perpendicular to Lone Mountain. Digging the inside edges into the groomed snow, he expertly glided to a stop. Slowly, he inhaled the freezing Montana air, reducing his heart rate as he'd been taught as a SEAL.

He smiled.

Once again, he had mastered the mountain. He gazed at the peak and traced the path he'd skied from 11,166 feet down to 7,400 feet at the Madison Base Area. Dropping into Stillwater Bowl through the longest of the double black diamond entries, he'd dodged trees through Sundance Hollow before shooting across the intermediate slopes to finish on Pine Marten. He preferred the less crowded side of Big Sky Resort.

Damn, it had been an invigorating ride.

Isaac burrowed through several layers of clothing and gloves to check the large face of his military watch. He had just enough time to peel off his ski gear and drive to the locals' bar on the outskirts of the high-priced resort town. He couldn't wait to see Peter "Pipes" Eastwood again.

They'd grown up together in the same small mountain town, playing football in the fall and baseball in the spring together. They'd hunted everything from elk to rabbits but agreed that nothing tasted better than fresh-caught trout fried in a cast iron pan over an open fire. When the Navy recruiter showed up their senior year, they both decided to see the world. Their scores on the range and agility on the obstacle course made them candidates for SEAL training. Together, they'd made it through BUD/S training but were separated once they'd reached Virginia Beach.

The SEAL community was quite small and closed to outsiders, even after they left the Navy.

Fifteen minutes later, Isaac hit the lock button on the key fob to the brand-new Land Rover provided to him for this assignment. He scanned the parking lot filled with well-worn four-wheel-drive vehicles a decade old and grimaced. Guardian Security was a first-class company all the way, and he loved working for them, but the vehicle screamed, *Rob me. I'm a tourist.* Thankfully, the heavily tinted windows hid all the new gear he'd purchased the day before for this assignment. He groaned when he thought about shopping tomorrow to outfit a pampered princess with the equipment she'd need for Plan B.

But first, a beer and some good food with an old friend.

Isaac loved Buck's Place. He and his buddies had been regulars his junior and senior years of high school, stopping in after a long, cold day of running ski lifts for minimum wage at the popular winter destination.

Employees weren't allowed to mingle with resort guests, not that they ever wanted to spend time with the rich and famous or their over-indulged children. The dingy bar had been one of the few places they could get a hot meal without accusing glances.

Crossing the snow-covered gravel parking lot, Isaac automatically scanned for threats and then chastised himself. He was no longer in the desert, and this was snow, not sand. Isaac held the door open wide, allowing the bright sunshine to illuminate the small, enclosed porch. His gaze immediately swept the area for threats before he stepped inside. Given his new job, perhaps some cautious habits should be kept.

Scuffing the soles of his boots on the thick wiry mat to remove any remnant of snow embedded in the deep tread gave his eyes a few seconds to adjust to the faint light before he closed them. The bar would be darker yet.

Entering a dimly lit room could temporarily blind a man...and get him killed. Some lessons were learned the hard way.

Isaac shoved the memories of house-to-house searches in war-torn countries aside. This was Buck's Place. He was safe and back in Montana.

His first thought as he stepped through the well-worn door was that not much had changed in the eight years he'd been gone. The menagerie of elk, sheep, and deer trophies that filled every square foot of wall space to the fourteen-foot open beam ceiling had expanded. All had been locally shot, most by regular patrons. Interspersed throughout were prize-worthy fish expertly restored by a local taxidermist.

In the middle of the afternoon, there weren't many people in the bar. Pete was easy to spot. He sat with another dark-haired man at a table in the back, both wearing the dark green uniform of national forest rangers. Their table was close to an emergency exit, where they could see everything and everyone. It was where Isaac would have chosen to sit had he arrived first.

Both men rose as Isaac approached. Pete immediately pulled him in for a smack on the back and a bro hug.

"So damned good to see you." He pointed to the man next to him but extended his hand. "Isaac, I'd like you to meet my partner, Mark Hamner. Call him Grinch."

"You hate Christmas?" Isaac asked as they shook.

"Not anymore since my boots now live on U.S. soil." The man who stood an inch taller than Isaac shrugged. "Spending my third Christmas in Fuckastan, I was not a happy camper. My Green Beret Alpha team gave me the new name and it stuck."

"Army." Isaac grinned at Peter.

"Yeah, but we don't hold that against him."

All three men sat down at the old scarred wooden table.

The middle-aged waitress showed up, and Isaac eyed the beers sitting in front of the others. He wasn't going to be on duty for several hours, so he ordered his favorite local brew and a small pizza. When she was gone, they all sat back in the sturdy wooden chairs.

"Looks like you two are settling into civilian life." Isaac's gaze bounced between his old friend and new acquaintance.

When Mark's eyes met Pete's, they both grinned as though they knew a secret.

"A good job and a hot woman in a soft bed to come home to every night, what's not to like?" Mark picked up his bottle of beer and took a sip.

"Hey, asshole, that's my sister you're talking about." Pete glared at the slightly larger man.

"You married Carrie?" Isaac remembered Pete's

little sister as a junior high cheerleader. She was cute but she was his buddy's little sister, thus off-limits. Besides, there were plenty of well-developed varsity cheerleaders to occupy his time.

Mark smiled as he set his bottle back on the table. "Yep. I'm the luckiest man around. Just another perk of living here."

Pete focused intense brown eyes on Isaac. "That reminds me, I was serious when I suggested you join the Forest Service." He held up one hand. "Before you get started, I know and understand why you wouldn't want to live here. But now that you're back, you might change your mind. We're always in need of more men, especially with your training and local expertise. Offer is always open."

There was no fucking way Isaac would ever choose to live in Montana again. He couldn't get away from this place fast enough at eighteen. He was only back now out of necessity.

"Thanks, Pete, but I'm only here for a few days." At least Isaac hoped that was the truth. Since he didn't have enough details about his next assignment yet, he wasn't sure how long he'd have to remain in the area. He didn't like being this close to his father's home and the past he thought he'd left far behind.

Refusing to go down that path, Isaac needed to pave the way for Guardian Security. "If you decide to quit being a mountain man and join civilization, your skills are always needed at Guardian."

"What is it exactly that you're doing up here?" Pete leaned his elbows on the table. Lowering his voice he asked, "Can you tell me?"

He wasn't on any kind of a top-secret mission, at least as far as he knew. "My client's parents have used Guardian Security services for years. Seems their little princess has pissed off someone, and they want her protected for a while." He shrugged. "That's all I know right now. I'm supposed to get more details later tonight from someone higher up the food chain."

Pete cocked one eyebrow. "So, her folks sent her to Big Sky, Montana?"

"I guess they own a place here and thought it was far enough away from Atlanta that she'd be safe." Isaac smiled. "I could handle an assignment skiing my ass off for a couple days on somebody else's dime."

Although working for Guardian Security paid extremely well, lift tickets at the exclusive resort were pricey. Thanks to a few old high school friends he'd run into last night at this very bar, he was able to sneak onto the chairlift before the slopes actually opened. First tracks in fresh powder was one of the few good memories Isaac had growing up in the rural mountains. He'd spent his morning acclimating to the high altitude by getting in as many runs as possible.

"You'd better hope she knows how to ski better

than the movie star wannabes that live in the huge mansions on the resort slopes." Mark scowled. "I didn't know anybody could be so damned uncoordinated. I've picked up bony asses off the slopes so times I lost count. They should give me a red jacket and put me on ski patrol."

Pete burst into a laugh. "I wish I could've been there to see Carrie's face. My sister has a jealous streak."

"She's the one who stopped me 'to help the poor lady' each and every time." Marcus grinned. "After about the fifth time she watched some woman hanging all over me trying to get her skis back under her, Carrie just skied on past any other damsels in distress."

Pete chuckled. "Sounds like something my little sister would do."

After a moment, Mark's whole face transformed. "Yeah. She's got a mean streak in her. As long as it's not pointed at me, I'm golden."

"Any idea how long you'll be here?" Pete asked.

"If I'm that lucky, a few days. Maybe a week." Isaac admitted, "I'd like a short assignment."

"Then back to Atlanta?" Pete finished his beer and set the bottle on the table.

The men remained silent as the waitress slid their pizzas in front of them and asked if they wanted another beer. They all rejected the offer in favor of the full water glasses on the table.

"I may take a day or two and drop in on my Uncle Samuel." Isaac hadn't seen his mother's brother in almost a year, since they had finished the inside of the cabin on the backside of Lone Mountain. He missed the grouchy old man who had given him the few good memories he had of his childhood after his mother had died of ovarian cancer when he was eight.

"Uncle Bullshit?" Pete said with a smile.

"Samuel Bull Tail," Isaac corrected, although he often wondered if half the stories he'd heard over the years were real. He'd seen the Ranger patch on Uncle Samuel's U.S. Army uniform and had once donned the green beret and marched around the small home he preferred to the large, two-story ranch house he'd grown up in.

"I've heard that name a lot," Mark noted. "Are you Crow?"

"According to Uncle Samuel, yes." Isaac bit into what had to be some of the best pizza in the world.

"We had a few Crow and Northern Cheyenne in our school, but most went to the schools closer to the reservations," Pete said before winding a long string of cheese around the tip of his slice. He stared at Isaac before taking a bite. "You kinda look like them."

"Yeah, I take after my mom." And thank God for that. He was happy to look into the mirror every day and see his mother's high cheekbones and square jaw. Facing a reminder of his father carved into his own face day after day would be more than Isaac could bear. Not having to shave off beard stubble each morning was another sign of his true ancestry. A heritage his father vehemently denied.

"Do you have other family in the area?" Mark's question was innocent given that Isaac rarely spoke of his father. Pete knew the story, or at least part of it.

Since Pete had been on a mission in Iraq while Isaac's platoon was training in Alaska, he had seemed to know what Isaac needed upon him returning from his first mission to the sandbox. They had hit every bar in Virginia Beach and fucked several base bunnies before needing to sober up to resume training Monday morning. Isaac would be forever thankful for the way Pete had looked out for him during those first transitional days back on base. He'd been pretty fucked-up.

Mark looked at him expectantly, but it was Pete's gaze that bored deep.

Isaac couldn't lie under his friend's scrutiny. "Yes, but I won't be going there." He hoped they both understood the double meaning of his words. He had no intention of returning to the hell he'd lived in before escaping into the Navy, nor would he be discussing his father, stepmother, and half-siblings with the two of them.

Just before his tenth birthday, his father had shown up on their large Montana ranch with a young, blonde-haired, blue-eyed bitch who treated

Isaac like a house servant. She'd popped out three little girls before finally giving his father a second son during Isaac's senior year in high school.

He was embarrassed at the seventeen-year difference. No teenage boy wanted to think of his parents still having sex while he was discovering the ecstasy of orgasms with girls. Some had accused Isaac of knocking up a girl he dated his entire junior year—whose family had moved away over the summer—claiming his father and step-mother were raising the baby as their own.

Just another reason to leave small-town life.

Isaac couldn't wait to graduate and get the hell out of the Montana mountains.

But now he was back, temporarily, and working because he had a unique knowledge of the area.

Deep in his pocket, Isaac's phone vibrated. Voice-mail or email, either way, he knew it was from his office. Digging out his phone, he glanced at the email showing it had an attachment.

Holding up his phone, Isaac declared, "Sorry, guys, duty calls."

All three men stood.

"We need to get back across the mountains," Pete announced. "Take care of yourself. I understand we're about to get dumped on."

"Yeah, they're calling for another three feet starting tomorrow afternoon." Mark grabbed the jacket from the back of his chair and stuffed his arms down the sleeves.

"It's been a while since you've lived in high country." Pete slipped on his parka. "I know you went to cold-weather training like we all did, but you've been away from life in the snow for several years."

Before he would allow the lecture he knew was coming, Isaac said, "I haven't forgotten anything I learned growing up here."

Pete nodded. "Stay safe."

It had taken a few minutes for the three of them to pay their bills and say their final farewells. Isaac had just turned the key in the ignition when his phone rang. All the caller ID showed was Guardian Security.

"Isaac Snow," he announced to the caller.

"Good afternoon, Isaac. This is Alex Wolf."

Isaac sat up straighter in his seat. Although he'd met the owner and managing partner of Guardian Security once before, he was the last man Isaac expected on the other end of the line.

"Sir, what can I do for you?" Isaac couldn't imagine what the man at the top of the multimillion-dollar company wanted.

"Have you had an opportunity to look at the files on Hannah Kader?"

Well, hell. He'd only received them about five minutes ago. "No, sir. I was not alone when I received the email, but I intend to study them once I am back in my hotel room." And what a room it was. Guardian Security had arranged for a suite for him to stay in while at Big Sky. He'd never been in such a fancy hotel room in his life. The large living room had a wet bar tucked into one corner with crystal highball and wine glasses. It was separated from the bedroom by double doors. There was a full kitchen, not that Isaac was expected to cook because room service was available 24/7. The flatscreen TV was about the same size as his at home, huge by most standards, but he didn't have a gas fireplace that turned on with a remote, or a jetted tub next to a shower big enough for three. To top it off, he could ski from the patio onto the slopes. He was living the luxurious life he'd only seen from a distance as a Montana rancher's kid.

"Let me fill you in on what has happened since those reports were compiled." Alex's tone was direct and to the point.

Isaac wondered if the parents of the pampered princess were best friends with the owner of the company.

Deciding he needed to see the information sooner rather than later, Isaac headed toward the hotel.

"What do you know about Hannah Kader?" Alex asked.

"Absolutely nothing, except I'm here to protect her," Isaac admitted. Then, to reassure his boss, he added, "But I will know everything in that file as soon as I get back to my room. Should her name ring a bell?"

Alex paused for a long minute before he answered. "No, but for some reason, ISIS wants her dead."

CHAPTER 2

HANNAH KADER KNEW HE WAS HEADED HER WAY A FULL minute before the tall man with the scraggly brown mustache and beard started up the sidewalk. Standing back several feet from the window, hiding in the shadows of the house, she focused the long camera lens. His skin tone was wrong to be Middle Eastern, but it wouldn't be the first time ISIS had recruited an all-American-looking young man.

Click. Click.

She sharpened the edges of his face, wishing she could see his eyes behind the reflective glasses.

Click. Click.

His swagger was confident, almost cocky as he strode the fifteen feet to the steps. He certainly wasn't trying to be stealthy in that bright yellow jacket. Although the reflective striping required for serious backcountry exploration was designed into the outer jacket, the coat had not been purchased off the rack at a local boutique. It was too high-tech.

She scanned his body for weapons. So much could be hidden under the large parka, including multiple handguns, knives, and even a submachine gun.

He constantly rotated his head from side to side. She was sure he'd mentally logged every vehicle on the street and could accurately describe the couple and their two children next door playfully having a snowball fight.

She could.

Hannah moved to observe him on the porch. She took another few pictures as he stomped the snow off his boots. She touched the button to send her shots directly to her computer then slid the camera into a duffel bag on the dining table.

Withdrawing her Sig Sauer .45 caliber, she stepped quietly across the thick-padded living room carpet onto the tile at the front door. She was already looking through the peephole when he rang the bell.

"Who are you, and what do you want?" Her voice was rough from lack of use the past two weeks. She had limited her calls to her parents, primarily texting once a day using the throwaway cell phone she had picked up at a gas station when she had flown into Bozeman.

"Ma'am, I'm Isaac Snow from Guardian Security's

Atlanta Center." He slipped off his glove and reached into his pocket.

She immediately brought the gun up. She was pretty sure he couldn't fire a bullet through the solid core front door, but a single shot would shatter the glass in the windows three feet away. He could be inside in seconds.

Instead, he held an identification card up to the peephole.

She liked that even less because it blocked her view and she couldn't see what he was doing. Stepping to the side, Hannah flipped the deadbolt and opened the door a crack. The chain lock hung loosely at chin level.

"I'm here to meet Hannah Kader." The man slid a business card toward her.

She snatched the small paper from his fingers and slammed the door shut. The black and gold business card had the words Guardian Security, Inc. underneath the name Isaac Snow. There was no title distinguishing him as a manager, owner, or peon. Nothing. In the lower right corner were an Atlanta address and a phone number.

Hannah peered through the peephole to watch the man turn his back to the door and take a selfie.

What. The. Hell?

Sure, his rugged good looks were accentuated in that orange parka, but was the man that vain and so bored he decided to use her silence for selfies? And why the hell would he photograph himself on her porch?

He lowered his phone, his thumbs flying over the screen as he turned back around.

Damn. He was sending the pictures to someone.

Hannah quickly debated between calling 911 or the phone number on the card.

Was he texting pictures of her parents' home in Big Sky to a local ISIS cell, pointing out where she was? She glanced through the living room windows to the street looking to see if reinforcements were on their way to kidnap her. Or to kill her.

At no sign of traffic, Hannah wanted to kick her own butt. ISIS didn't knock on the door and introduce themselves.

With a sigh, she reconsidered his actions. Maybe he was sending a picture to his girlfriend to prove that he was at work.

She compared the phone number on the card with the one her father had given her to call in case of an emergency. It was the same. With a sigh of relief, she dialed.

"Guardian Security, Atlanta Center. Is this an emergency?"

The unexpected question gave her pause. No. A strange man at her front door was not an emergency as far as she could tell. He might even be the one she'd expected, but Hannah had learned in a mud block hovel in Syria that you don't even trust those who you consider friends.

"Hello. Not exactly an emergency, but I need to confirm that one of your agents...employees...whatever you call them...is in fact the man standing at my door." That didn't come out as smooth as Hannah had hoped. She was obviously more shaken up than she'd admitted to herself.

She peered through the peephole at the man on the porch. He stood back so she could see him head to toe, his gloved hands clasped in front of him, feet spread shoulder-width apart. He turned his head side to side then he stared at the door as though he could see through it.

She quickly took a step back.

The sound of tapping computer keys over the phone line had stopped. "Ma'am, I see you are at—"

When the man in Atlanta spoke her address, fear shot through Hannah. They knew exactly where she was. Her eyes immediately darted to the back door. It took thirty-five seconds to reach the vehicle she had parked a block away. Everything she needed was in the duffel bag that lay unzipped on the dining table.

"Is this Hannah Kader?"

She jerked at the sound of her name.

"Ms. Kader. Are you still there?"

She looked at the phone in her hand as though it was about to bite her.

"Ms. Kader. Hannah Kader. Please respond or I

will call the local police and direct them to your home."

No. Sirens and flashing blue lights would be a beacon for anyone searching for her, not to mention the call over open airwaves.

Taking a deep breath, she exhaled slowly, wrestling her fears under control. "I'm here. Thank you, but police are unnecessary." At least she hoped. "Is the man outside my door one of yours?"

Her phone dinged indicating a text.

"I have just sent you a picture of Isaac Snow, your personal protection arranged for by your parents. Please check your text." Efficient and calm would be the words Hannah would use to describe the man on the other end of the line.

Glancing down at the picture, Hannah smiled then lifted her gaze to the man standing on the porch. It was the selfie he had taken less than a minute ago.

Damn, these guys were good. She suddenly felt better about the entire situation.

Lifting the phone back to her ear, Hannah replied, "Yes, it's him. Thank you so much." She ended the call and slid the phone into her back pocket.

After releasing the chain, Hannah opened the door. "Mr. Snow, won't you come in, please."

As he stepped inside, he removed the knit cap and ran long fingers through nearly black hair, removing any remnants of hat head. Then he took off the reflective sunglasses and tucked them into the collar of his sweater. When his gaze met hers, Hannah took a step back. Those deep brown eyes were decades older than the face of the man who stood only three feet away.

"Hannah Kader, I presume?" There was a hint of annoyance in his voice. His gaze scanned her body and stopped on the gun in her hand which she held next to her thigh.

"Yes." She waggled the business card. "Isaac Snow, I'd like to take a good look at that identification, please."

With his gaze still pinned on the gun, he slid off one glove and reached into the parka pocket. He held out his corporate identification. Maintaining her distance, she scrutinized the picture, glancing between the man and the photograph several times. ID pictures never did anyone justice. He was much more handsome in real life. Or maybe it was just the testosterone-enriched aura he exuded.

"Thank you." Hannah shifted her weight, putting even more space between the two of them. "I've never had a bodyguard before." She'd never needed one. She knew how to kick ass and take names all on her own. She didn't need some man to take care of her.

A year of training by some of the fiercest fighters in the world, the Kurdish Peshmerga, had taught Hannah how to protect herself. Fighting in the all-female YPJ Battalion of the Syrian People's Protection Unit the following year had shown her how to protect those weaker than her in ISIS-claimed areas of Syria and Iraq.

Hannah wondered how much Isaac Snow knew about her. "So, where do we start?"

"You can start by handing me that gun." His gaze glanced down then right back to meet hers.

There was no way in hell she was going to let go of her Sig. It had saved her life multiple times. "Not happening, big boy."

The right side of his lips twitched. "I take it you know how to use that P220?"

She grinned. "It's a P320, and yes. Would you like me to give you a skills demonstration, or perhaps you need a handgun lesson?" During her time in the Middle East, Hannah had taught hundreds of young women how to use pistols, rifles, submachine guns, and even rocket launchers. But the look in his eyes told her he could pick up any weapon and use it efficiently.

Isaac slid out of his boots. "Just don't point it toward me. You'll find one looking right back at you. I'd appreciate it if you'd put that thing away. I'm here to protect you. Not kill you."

Hannah slid the gun into the holster at the small of her back. "Satisfied?"

Without acknowledgment, he announced, "We need to secure the house and then we'll talk." He started with the window next to the front door, checking the locks and the area he could see outside. He then lowered the blackout shades, encasing them in near darkness.

She followed him, turning on lamps. Hannah had preferred to sit in the shadows and be able to see out, but Isaac's concern was obviously the opposite. He didn't want anyone to be able to see in.

From the middle of the living room, Hannah watched Isaac prowl through the house like a cat on silent feet as he checked out every room, every window, and every door. She followed him upstairs and to the basement. He wouldn't find anything because she had done her own sweep less than an hour ago. Finished, he went directly to the coat rack in the foyer.

As he shucked off the parka, all Hannah could do was stare. Muscles rippled under the dark green sweater that highlighted the jade ring around his brown, nearly black irises. The man was built. She'd worked for years in the desert with soldiers who were in excellent shape, but most were on the thin side and looked like long-distance runners. Isaac had broad, well-defined shoulders and the thick thighs of a swimmer.

She couldn't help herself, she had to know, "Are you a SEAL?" She saw the ever so brief hesitation in his movement as he hung his coat.

"I work for Guardian Security." He turned toward

her. "But I was a SEAL. That shouldn't make a difference. I'm here to protect you, and I'm completely able to keep you safe."

Hannah certainly hoped so. According to her brother, the bounty for her—dead or alive—was now up to $500,000 U.S. Aziz's family certainly wanted revenge.

CHAPTER 3

HANNAH KADER WAS NOT WHAT ISAAC HAD EXPECTED, especially after Alex Wolf told him ISIS was after her. Even though Guardian Security often worked directly for the United States Special Operations Command, none of his boss's high-ranking contacts could tell him why the terrorists wanted her dead.

To Isaac, Hannah seemed more like the girl next door than a threat to the Middle Eastern extremist regime.

Slightly wavy, dark brown hair draped just beyond her shoulders, but it was the huge Bambi eyes and full lips that held Isaac's attention. She reminded him of Angelina Jolie. Their build was even similar. He held back a smile as he thought of Hannah dressed like the *Lara Croft* movie character in a tight-fitting skin suit with weapons strapped to her thighs and across her back.

His cock twitched at the picture he painted in his mind. Hell of a time for his libido to decide to reawaken. He'd gone nearly a year without a real hard-on. Coming home from a tough mission to find his fiancée dead on the bathroom floor was a real cock blocker.

Before the constant regret could overtake his every thought, Isaac returned his attention to the woman in front of him. He mentally measured her for skis and the gear they would need tomorrow morning. She was about five-feet, seven-inches, maybe a hundred and thirty pounds. She looked fit.

"You seem to be in pretty good shape," Isaac commented.

"I have to be for my job." She shifted her weight. "Can we sit down like civilized adults?" She walked into the living room and sat on one end of the couch then popped back up. "I'm sorry, I truly do have manners. Would you like something to drink?"

Without waiting for his answer, her long, shapely legs took her to the refrigerator. The yoga pants she wore showed off strong thighs and calves, not to mention one of the nicest asses Isaac had ever seen.

"I have sports drinks, flavored water, beer, several kinds of juice, and milk." She looked over her shoulder expectantly.

He was on duty so beer was out of the question. "Gatorade would be great." As an afterthought, he added the word, "Please."

With the flavored water in one hand, she stuck out her arm, practically shoving the sports drink into his abdomen on her way back to the couch. "Come and sit. I can't stand you looming over me."

Isaac sat in a chair several feet away from Hannah. Unscrewing the cap, he took in the beautiful house. The exposed timbers were very typical of Big Sky homes, as was a huge stone fireplace. Windows filled the side facing Lone Mountain from floor to the ceiling peak twenty-five feet above. He had closed the drapes covering the three sets of sliding glass doors that opened to a deck that ran the width of the house but the other windows had no coverings.

"Nice place," Isaac noted. "I take it this is a winter vacation home for your parents?" He took a long pull on his drink. Growing up in the area, he was quite familiar with beautiful homes that were only used for a week or two in the winter. The rest of the year they remained empty or rented through one of the local real estate agencies.

"We've often spent holidays here, even Fourth of July." Defensively, she added, "My parents have very high-pressure jobs. They come here to get away from the big city atmosphere and relax."

"What do they do?" Isaac hoped the question would keep her talking. They needed to develop a familiarity since they were going to be stuck together for at least a week, longer if Homeland Security couldn't pin down the ISIS cell soon.

"My father works for the Center for Disease Control and my mother is an emergency room physician at Emory Hospital." She lifted her chin as though to say, *See, their work is very stressful.*

Isaac was tempted to counter by telling her, *My father is a rancher and my stepmother is his trophy wife who doesn't know how to do anything except spend his hard-earned money.* And damn, Isaac knew exactly how hard it was to earn money raising cattle and the physical labor required.

Instead, he asked, "Do you know how to ski?"

She cocked her head and raised one eyebrow. "I learned to ski when I was three. I'm a long way from competition level, but Stillwater Bowl is one of my favorite runs. In case you don't know—"

"I'm familiar with every trail at this resort," Isaac cut her off.

"You're a local?" Hannah asked, bottle of water halfway to her luscious lips.

"No." He didn't want her forming an opinion based on where he grew up. He may have spent the first eighteen years of his life in and around these mountains, but the last eight years in the Navy, six of those as a SEAL, had made him the man he was now. "I already told you, I live in Atlanta."

Changing the subject, Isaac asked, "Have you ever done any backcountry skiing?"

Hannah's whole face lit up and it was as though a beam of sunlight had cut through the darkness of the enclosed house. "It's one of my favorite things to do here at Big Sky. Are we going Alpine touring?"

"It's a possibility." Isaac had planned for several scenarios. One of his backup plans was to take Hannah to his Uncle Samuel's remote cabin. Plan A, though, was to hang out in this house and test her skiing skills in case they had to move to Plan B, while they waited for Homeland Security to do their job. The house was as secure as any Atlanta antebellum mansion. Guardian Security had eyes and ears inside and out, constantly monitored by men he knew well.

"Can we go tomorrow morning?" Excitement exuded from her. "I love skiing on virgin snow. The resort has a helicopter that can drop us off on top of the mountain and they have a car service to pick us up when we're finished."

Isaac's experience with helicopter drops onto snow was quite different. His SEAL team had trained in Alaska for nearly six weeks. They had fast-roped out of choppers and were forced to make their way back to base camp carrying nearly one hundred pounds of gear on their backs. Several times the trip took days, always in below-freezing weather. It wasn't a pleasant experience, even for a man raised in the Montana mountains.

"They also have a guide service." Hannah smiled broadly. "We should ask for Samuel. He's this big ole bear of a man—salt and pepper beard halfway down his chest, his face looks like tanned leather, and he has the best stories about the Indians that once roamed this area. Screw up, and he won't hesitate to yell at you, but underneath he's a teddy bear."

So that's how his uncle had afforded the high-end amenities he'd put in the cabin. Sly old goat. Uncle Samuel had been a hunting guide for years, but that gig only lasted a few months. He'd often complained about clueless city fishermen who flew in for one week to wade in the area's Blue Ribbon Rivers or pristine lakes, fully expecting to leave with a trophy trout, salmon, or bass so they could brag to their friends back home. Isaac would bet good money the old fart was raking in thousands showing tourists a good time tromping around the backcountry, too.

"We won't be needing a guide, but I'll keep that in mind," Isaac reassured Hannah. "So, do you have your own backcountry gear?"

She bounced to her feet. "We store it down in the basement. Follow me."

Oh, yes. He'd follow that pretty little ass almost anywhere.

He gave himself a mental slap. He was there to protect that pretty little ass, not tap it.

While securing the house, he had seen a room filled with everything from downhill skis to four-season sleeping bags. She led him past the small downstairs kitchen, the pool table, and two more bedrooms before reaching the storage area at the far end.

"You might want to reconsider hiring Samuel." Hannah pulled a large plastic bin with her name on it from the shelf. "He took my brother and me on a three-day, two-night backcountry excursion. It was outstanding. We saw elk and sheep, and I caught my first fish in a pool at the bottom of a waterfall. Best trout I've ever eaten."

Fresh trout was one of Isaac's absolute favorite meals. He wondered if Hannah would be interested in going out for a bite to eat. He hadn't seen his kind of food in her refrigerator. He had to be careful, but he seriously doubted anyone from ISIS knew her location. She'd already be kidnapped or dead if they did.

Hannah popped the top off the bin. She withdrew a pair of ski skins and pointed toward the wall. "These fit my telemark skis and you can see my bindings were built for backcountry touring."

Isaac was impressed. Her equipment wasn't just high-end, it was high-tech, even though it was a few years old. The skis and poles also looked as though they had been used, but not abused. He hated when people spent good money on great equipment and then didn't take care of it.

She lifted out a red, waterproof bag labeled *Avalanche* and opened it. "Transceiver, reflector, probe, extra insulation layer." She named each object as she pulled it out.

"Have you had avalanche training?" Isaac asked.

With a knowing grin, she lifted that pointy chin of hers. "I've been through Level III Certification courses at the American Avalanche Institute." She leaned her forearms on the box. "I love this shit. I'd rather be all alone, trudging up a hill, my thighs and calves burning, than dodging novice skiers on packed snow. Don't get me wrong, I love the speed and adrenaline rush of downhill skiing, but walking through fresh powder, listening to nature all around me...it's like a religious experience."

Isaac completely understood. When things had gotten rough at home, he'd taken off for a walk in the woods, no matter what time of year. Sometimes that meant cross-country skis, other times snowshoes, and summertime meant boots. Nature had a distinct calming effect on him. As a teenager, he and Uncle Samuel would walk for miles in silence, simply absorbing the very essence of nature.

"I know exactly what you mean," he admitted. Changing the subject, which he seemed to have to do a lot with Hannah, he looked into the bin and asked, "Do you have a backpack?"

She stood. When she stretched to reach the top shelf, her forearm was exposed. Was that a tattoo of a feather? He wondered what other tattoos she had... and where. His gaze passed over her body. So many interesting places she could have ink. He could picture himself sliding off that loose-fitting shirt and peeling down the yoga pants that fit her like a second skin, checking every inch of her body for tattoos.

His cock became very interested in the idea of a naked Hannah.

Don't go there, sailor. She's a client. He stood and reached over her head grabbing the dark blue back-pack. The coconut scent of her shampoo hit him just before the heat of her body radiated into his chest.

"This one?" His voice sounded gruff in the small room. He stepped back and the entire front of his body cooled, missing her next to him. Ignoring his erection, he suggested, "Let's get this packed so it's ready when we decide to go backcountry."

"Is that what we're going to do tomorrow?" Hannah put the subzero sleeping bag in the very bottom, just as he would've done.

"No, I think we'll warm up our legs with some downhill first." Isaac really needed to determine her skill level. He knew far too many men and women who could talk a good game but when faced with the challenges of the mountain, they just couldn't handle it.

Hannah started to secure the top of the backpack when Isaac noticed the avalanche sack. "You forgot this."

"No, I put it in this outside pocket." She took it

from him and started to place it in the zippered area behind her right hip.

"You should put it up here." Isaac grabbed for the bag, but she clutched it to her chest.

"This is where I learned to carry it and it's where I'm going to put it." Hannah glared at him. "It's my damn pack, and I'll put everything where I know exactly where it is, and I can reach it."

He relented. *Choose your battles*, Uncle Samuel used to always say.

Isaac visually inspected the backpack. "What's this?" He pointed to a hard nylon tubing that would sit against her body. He'd never seen anything like that before.

"That's an avalanche airbag." She hoisted the backpack onto her shoulders. "All I have to do is pull on this." Hannah indicated a tab on her left shoulder. "It automatically inflates from my hips to about two feet above my head. Side bags protect my shoulders and hold my head securely."

That was the coolest thing Isaac had ever seen. He immediately Googled it on his phone. When he clicked on the video, Hannah stood so close her breasts touched his biceps every time she took a breath. For several minutes, they watched people skiing and snowboarding on extremely steep slopes getting caught in avalanches, then inflating the airbags.

"I need one of those," he declared just above a whisper.

"This brand is the best," Hannah pointed to her backpack. "I've done extensive research." She glanced up to the top shelf. "Grab that red backpack. I bought one for my brother when I got this one. He won't mind if you use his. He's far too busy with his residency at Johns Hopkins to make it out here this winter."

Isaac gazed at her. She seemed so open and honest with her responses, caring for his safety, that he had to remind himself that she was being hunted. "Thanks. I appreciate that. Let me run out to my SUV and grab mine to transfer everything into this one."

"While you take care of that, I'm going to make some spaghetti for supper." As they both turned to head up the steps, she added, "Don't expect much. My cooking skills are limited to boiling water and heating a jar of spaghetti sauce in the microwave."

Isaac smiled. "Then I'll cook breakfast. I make a mean omelet." The idea of making breakfast after spending the night with a woman took on a new reality.

CHAPTER 4

Hannah couldn't sleep.

After she made a passable supper of spaghetti, Isaac had taken a phone call outside and brought in his bags. He'd transferred his backcountry gear into her brother's backpack and then set it next to hers. She was excited about Alpine touring with him.

Although she enjoyed skiing the slopes at Big Sky, the thousands of people who flocked to the resort made her nervous. She much preferred cornflower-blue skies, pure white newly fallen snow, and the fresh scent of the tall pine trees that created a circle around the base of the mountain.

She rolled to her side and readjusted her pillow. Through her open bedroom door, she heard Isaac's soft snoring and wondered what he wore to bed, especially after what she'd seen a few hours ago.

During her college days, she often slept naked. In

Syria, she had spent her nights hunting ISIS extremists and slept during the day in the busy encampment filled with other female members of the YPJ. There was usually a battalion of men from the Syrian People's Protection Units located on the same base. She had learned to sleep in much of her uniform, boots next to her bed, ready to move at a moment's notice. Since she had returned to the United States and was told about the threat on her life, she had been sleeping in clothes she could easily escape in, which often meant yoga pants and a T-shirt.

Hannah rolled to her back and listened to the slow, rhythmic breathing coming from the room across the hall.

He was the reason she couldn't sleep.

Although there were three bedrooms on this floor, the master was at the end of the hall. When Hannah had arrived a week ago, she'd selected her bedroom based on security reasons. She had multiple exits available to her, she could go up or down depending on her situation assessment, and it was central to the entire house so she could keep an eye on everything at the same time. Besides, sleeping in her parents' bedroom had a definite ick factor to it.

There wasn't a problem until Isaac insisted on taking the bedroom across from hers. That meant sharing a bathroom. Hannah moved all her personal items to the master bathroom. That felt like less of an intrusion on her parents' private space than if he were using it. Besides, she loved their dual showerheads.

Cotton abraded cotton as Isaac rolled over across the hall. The thought of him sleeping so close made her girl parts tingle again.

Several hours ago, she had seen his magnificent body in nothing but a towel riding low on narrow hips. She had almost reached her bedroom door after brushing her teeth and washing her face in her parents' ensuite when Isaac stepped out of the smaller bathroom. All she could do was stand and gape. She couldn't stop looking at well-defined chest muscles under a smattering of dark hair. His flat nipples were nut brown and wrinkled like walnuts the longer she stared at him. She couldn't stop her gaze from wandering over six distinct ridges before finding the thin dense line of dark hair that led from his belly button to under the towel. Ho-ly hell. The man was built.

Her nipples had hardened, and she'd hoped the loose-fitting T-shirt hid them. It had been months since Hannah had sex, and just looking at Isaac made her wonder what sleeping with him would be like. She'd had a few lovers before Aziz, but they were boys, more interested in getting off than her orgasm. Not that Aziz had been all that concerned after the first few times.

While seducing her, he'd made sure she orgasmed before he slid inside her. Once they had been lovers for a while, he often came before she had time to get there. Looking back, she could now see that he was just using her for a quick fuck...and information.

She had been so young and naïve, believing they were in love. She'd trusted him, and that had turned out to be the biggest mistake of her life. And the lives of hundreds of young girls she was not able to save. Her love for him had blinded her.

That would never happen again. Never.

She pinched her eyes closed and fought back the truth. She might not live long enough to have to worry about falling in love again.

That was another reason she couldn't sleep.

She knew Isaac would protect her, if by some rare possibility Aziz's family actually found her and tried to kill her. Death would be preferred over kidnapping. She had seen the results of what ISIS soldiers had done to the young girls they'd captured. They would do even worse to her.

Hannah had to shove the pictures in her mind of abused teenage girls into the dark recesses before anger took over and she headed back to the Middle East to avenge the atrocities.

Her body was exhausted after being on alert constantly. She hadn't slept well in weeks. When she'd returned to the United States, she thought she had left all the troubles of the Middle East behind her. Then her mother had been attacked.

The Atlanta Police Department had called it a

mugging, an attempt to steal money or drugs as she'd left the hospital late one night. Her family knew differently. The men who'd beat the shit out of her mom had told her it was because she had given birth to such a rebellious daughter.

They had called her mother a whore because she touched men who were not her husband. The woman was an emergency room physician. Of course she touched men, several times a day. She also saved their lives, but the radicals didn't approve.

One of her mother's assailants chastised her because she wore American clothing and did not cover her body head to toe in an abaya. Hannah hated the attitude of extremist Muslims toward women. That was why she had joined the Syrian People's Protection Units, specifically the all-female YPJ.

She had been welcomed with open arms since she had been born in a Syrian refugee camp. She was also a citizen of the United States of America by birth. Her father had been born and raised in the USA, working for the CDC in Iraq when he'd met her mother. Even then, she had been an emergency room physician. The two had worked together and quickly fallen in love. Theirs was such a beautiful love story. Their affection for each other was evident every day in their touches, openly kissing in front of her and her brother. That was the kind of relationship she'd known all of her life and she wanted the same when she chose a husband.

Hannah thought she had followed in her mother's footsteps. Aziz had practically swept her off her feet. At twenty-one, she was thrilled to have captured the attention of the handsome Syrian army captain in his mid-thirties. Although she was not a virgin, she was definitely naïve when it came to a man as experienced as him.

Thanks to her American education, she had risen quickly through the officer ranks of the YPJ since women in the Middle East were given little opportunity for schooling. As they were the same rank, and Aziz's charismatic personality made him a favorite, their affair was shrugged off by senior officers.

Until she had revealed him as a traitor.

Smack. Smack.

The wind had kicked up and Hannah already knew that sound came from the external dryer vent. It had about scared her to death the first night she spent alone in the large house.

She heard the sheets rustle in the bedroom across the hall. Having Isaac so close was comforting and disturbing at the same time.

A board squeaked in the hallway, and Hannah reached under her pillow to grab her H&K mini submachine gun. She crept to the doorway and plastered herself against the wall. Peeping out, she saw

Isaac looking down the sights of a fifteen-round Sig Sauer.

"Isaac, it's just the dryer vent," Hannah said in a normal voice as she stepped out of her bedroom, gun nestled into her shoulder. *Trust no one* had been her motto since arriving in Syria four years ago. Only once had she let her guard down, and she was now being hunted because she'd trusted a man. Never again. Not even if he was supposed to protect her.

"Holy fuck!" Isaac lowered his gun. "I could have shot you. You should've stayed in your bedroom."

Hannah laughed as she let her gun drop down next to her thigh. "Let you wander all over this house clearing every room? I'll never get to sleep."

In the dim hallway lit by the half-moon reflecting off snow, she could see the tension ease the lines on his face. "Sometimes talking about your worries helps them go away."

A deep noise burst from within Hannah. It wasn't a chuckle but could have been perceived as one. "I don't think talking about the brother of the ISIS Caliphate is going to stop his family from hunting me down and trying to kill me." She let out a heavy sigh. "But maybe a strong drink will help me sleep."

Without turning on any lights, she walked to the wet bar in the corner of the living room. She laid her gun on the granite counter and removed a half-empty bottle of Maker's Mark bourbon from the glass shelf above. "Want one?" She turned the label toward Isaac.

He shook his head. "I'm on duty."

She grabbed a second glass. "I hate drinking alone. Besides, after that adrenaline rush you just had, you'll need something to bring you down to normal."

"You're right." Isaac was so close to her, she flinched. She hadn't heard him move. Damn, but she was off her game. If she wasn't more careful, she could end up dead.

She poured the golden liquid into a glass and handed it to him.

"I take it you know how to use that one, too?" He asked and held the glass to his nose, sniffing appreciatively.

Smiling as she poured the alcohol, she admitted, "I'm a damn good marksman with almost any weapon." She turned to face him. "But my favorite is my custom-made, Barrett 82A1. For a .50 caliber, it doesn't have much recoil and fits very nicely in a lightweight case. I can carry that little baby all day long, and all night."

She curled up in the corner of the couch tucking her feet under her, resting the small machine gun across her lap. She'd shocked him. She loved surprising men with her abilities. They always underestimated women.

Well, not always. Aziz had known exactly how to

play her. She had been the one to underestimate her foe.

Isaac had followed her to the seating area, and to her surprise, he settled at the other end of the couch after laying his gun on the coffee table in front of them.

"Why is ISIS after you?" Isaac had obviously decided to cut straight to the point.

After a moment of consideration, she decided she liked that. No games. No small talk. She decided to return the favor. "I'm sure you've heard of Abu Bakr al-Baghdadi, he's the Caliphate of ISIS."

Isaac nodded. "The self-professed direct descendent of Mohammed who, in 2014, declared himself the leader of the Islamic faithful because the Taliban was not fundamentalist enough for him. What about him?"

That was an excellent summary. Hannah was happy she didn't have to give him a Middle Eastern history lesson. She let out a long sigh. "Because of me, his brother is dead."

With her eyes now adjusted to the darkness, Hannah watched Isaac's jaw drop.

"You killed the heir apparent? The guy who would take over ISIS if we finally managed to kill al-Baghdadi?" Isaac closed his eyes and dropped his head on the back of the couch. "Oh, fuck," he said just above a whisper.

"I didn't shoot him," Hannah corrected. "I... All I

did… Oh, hell. It's a long story."

Isaac rolled his head to look down the couch at her. "I'm listening."

No. She'd already said too much. He knew ISIS was after her and it was his job to keep her safe. He didn't really need to know what an immature idiot she'd been. How easily she had been deceived and, without knowing it, had put thousands of others in danger.

"Maybe some other time." She downed the last of her bourbon, loving the burn from her throat to her stomach. She could almost feel the alcohol move throughout her body, warming and relaxing her at the same time. Suddenly she was tired. "I'm going to bed."

Isaac tossed back the last few drops in his glass. "I'm going to do a perimeter check." He stood, snatching the gun from the table, and stared at her. "Don't shoot me."

She couldn't stand the way he looked down at her, so she stood and straightened her shoulders. "I'll see you in the morning." She walked away. Without glancing back, she called out to him, "You promised to make breakfast. I like my coffee with two sugars. The real stuff, not that imitation shit."

When she turned into her bedroom, out of the corner of her eye, she saw him rinse their glasses and place them in the dishwasher.

Some woman had trained him well.

CHAPTER 5

Isaac didn't want anyone else to ride up the four-seat chairlift with them. He placed his pole so the woman next to him tilted over, falling into her friend.

"Come on, we can still make it." He and Hannah slid onto the loading platform, each reaching back to grab the rapidly approaching seat. Expertly dropping into position, Hannah pulled down the security bar.

"That wasn't very nice," she chastised, but then grinned. "I'm not sure I could've handled listening to Chatty Cathy and Ditzy Dottie another minute."

Isaac had to agree. The two women hadn't shut up since they'd skied into the long lift line seconds behind Hannah and him. If he had to listen to another word about designer purses, he was going to pull the gun from his back and give everyone around them relief from their high-pitched voices. Obviously, no one had taught those women skiing etiquette because they constantly ran their rental skis over the top of his brand-new Völkls. He had never been able to own such a fine pair of skis and would not have those if it weren't for his Guardian Security expense account.

The chair lifted them fifty feet above the ground. They were now completely alone and headed to the top of the mountain. Hannah had proven herself by dodging beginners on the novice slope, then again by gracefully handling an easy intermediate run. This time they would tackle a short black diamond before taking one of the more difficult intermediate slopes to the bottom. His confidence in her abilities had grown with each trip down.

Jumping right into what he needed to know, Isaac asked, "Have your parents owned the house we're staying in for very long?"

"Yes, and no." Hannah went on to explain. "When we were little, my parents and several other doctors from Atlanta went in together to buy the house under a corporation name. Eventually, my parents bought the others out. About two years ago, while my sister was clerking for a law office, she convinced my parents to reconfigure the corporation, removing their names." Hannah shrugged. "It all has to do with taxes, investments, and stuff I don't really care to learn. It's my parents' money. They can do whatever they want with it."

Clarifying, Isaac asked, "So there's no way this house could be traced to your parents?"

"As far as I know, it will appear as though my parents sold the house over a year ago. At least that's what my sister said when she suggested I come here." Her lips drew in a straight line. "They wanted to protect me and felt this was the safest place for me to be. That's when they contacted your office. They also stepped-up security for all of us."

Isaac looked at her for a long time. There was much more to that story, and he needed to know what specifically had happened. Something had forced her into hiding. "Tell me why."

Hannah looked down on the treetops as the lift bumped over several towers. "I'm sure you know about my mom's attack."

He nodded. "That was in the file."

"A few days after that, my dad didn't come home right after work like usual. We were all concerned that he'd gone after the men who had hurt Mom." She shook her head. "The opposite had happened. Dad had been jerked from his car in the parking lot at the CDC, beaten severely, then thrown in our front yard the next morning." She swallowed hard. "There was...they'd nailed a warning to his chest." Her voice broke.

Isaac wanted to take her in his arms and assure her that he would protect her with his life. But he couldn't do that. She was a client, and he had to remain professional, even though the look in her eyes was hot and needy the night before when he'd walked out of the shower.

Refocusing, he had to know what the note said. "Go on."

She took a deep breath of the frigid air and let it out slowly, a white stream condensing in front of her. "It was written in Arabic. *Turn over the Syrian whore, or next time he's dead.*"

"What did the police say about your father's assault and murder threat?" Isaac was furious. He had spent years fighting overseas to protect people back home, yet the threat to American lives had made it to the United States.

Hannah sniffed. "We never called the police. They didn't do shit when my mom was attacked, why should we expect anything different because it was my dad?"

The Guardian Security report hadn't included her father's kidnapping and assault. Isaac locked the details in his memory. He would have to add it when they got back to the house.

She watched a skier pass underneath them. "I had to leave to protect my family. Homeland Security wanted to put me into the Witness Protection Program, but my mother wouldn't allow it. Even while I was in Syria, we talked all the time. At least once a week we'd Skype just so we could see each other."

Isaac had a lot more questions, but they were almost to the end of the ride. Hannah lifted the safety bar and they scooted to the edge of the seat.

"You ready to hit Stillwater Bowl?" he asked.

Her grin was cocky. "Think you can keep up with me?"

"Anywhere, anytime." He shoved off the seat and glided down the ramp, following her to the side where they lowered their goggles. Snow had started falling on top of the mountain. He wove his thick mittens through the loops on his poles. He was good to go. He glanced over Hannah from the top of her helmet to her boots securely clamped into the bindings.

"Ready?" She called from behind the scarf that covered her nose and mouth and wound around her neck.

"After you," Isaac pulled his balaclava over his face, staving off the freezing wind. Gesturing toward the double black diamond sign, he followed her to the lip of the bowl before dropping nearly vertical.

She was as good as her word. Knees bent, skis nearly touching, she planted her poles like a pro and swung the tails of her skis side-to-side, controlling her descent down the steep sides.

As they crested the top, Hannah moved toward a copse of trees to get out of the biting wind. He skidded to a stop to join her.

She tucked her scarf under her chin and lifted her

goggles. Her radiant smile said everything. "That was awesome, but I'm getting hungry. Besides, after this morning's workout, I'm going to need a few minutes' rest. How about we head to the lodge for some lunch?"

"Sounds good to me." Isaac was always hungry, or so it seemed. "You want to take it easy on the way down?"

"Hell, no." She lowered her goggles once again and turned the tips of her skis toward the black diamond slope next to them.

Damn, what a woman!

Hannah had stopped a hundred feet from the lodge, so Isaac skied around to face her. She kept scanning the crowd.

"What's wrong?" He turned his head to see what she was looking at but her hand kept moving, sweeping her gaze carefully over the crowd. He automatically scanned the area for threats. There were so many people. Presumably, many were removing skis to head inside for some lunch while others were destined for the slopes.

"Can we eat somewhere else?" Hannah's eyes pinched together in the middle.

Isaac turned to check the mass of people. The back of his neck wasn't prickling, though. That was his early warning system. Too many times on missions when he was in danger, the fine hairs bristled and irritated. "Certainly, but I need to know what's making you nervous?"

"I just don't like big crowds." Her quiet admission seemed to pain her.

He understood. Making a quick decision, he pointed toward the backside of the rental building. "Follow me."

Pushing off hard with his poles to propel him up the slight rise, he headed to the familiar employee exit. Hidden from the crowd, he stepped out of his bindings and bent to lift his skis. He grabbed Hannah's also. "My truck is on the other side of this fence."

They exited through an almost secret gate into the employee parking lot. Clomping along in the stiff-footed ski boots, they crossed to his truck. As Isaac opened the back, he surveyed the many cases of firearms and ammunition. He felt a little ridiculous because to that point, he had seen no real threat to her life.

As she shucked off the nylon outer shell keeping her coat and pants dry, she smiled and her eyes grew wide. "Are we going to hit the range this afternoon?" She bumped his shoulder with hers. "You ready to get schooled on firearms?"

Hmm. Testing her ability with a gun might be a good idea. "Maybe." That's all the more Isaac would commit to.

After peeling off the first two layers and changing

into snow boots, they tossed all their outer gear into the back of the SUV. Isaac cautiously swept his gaze over the parking lot filled with rusty pickup trucks and four-wheel drives. All the employees of the ski resort worked from sunup to sundown, so he wasn't surprised that not a single vehicle entered or left. Relief washed over him as he pulled out of the parking lot.

Fifteen minutes later, they were in a small mom-and-pop bistro enjoying hot chili.

"The crowd bothered you." It was a statement, not a question. Isaac couldn't get the fear in her eyes out of his mind.

"There are too many people to watch for in a crowd." Hannah sipped her sweet tea.

He completely agreed. "Then it's a good thing we're going cross-country skiing this afternoon."

Hannah's warm smile did something to him deep inside. "Thank you." Her words were simple, but he could tell they were heartfelt.

"Oh, don't thank me yet. This isn't your typical cross-country ski area." One side of his mouth kicked up.

She set her glass down on the table. "Exactly what do you have in mind?"

"Are you familiar with the Olympic winter sport, biathlon?"

She sat back in her chair and crossed her arms, staring at him for a long minute. She gave him a wicked smile. "So now I'm going to be tested not only for my cross-country endurance, but also for my rifle skills. Care to place a wager on who shoots better?"

"I'm pretty deadly at fifty yards," he warned.

She leaned in. "I'm still lethal at fifteen hundred yards." She glanced around and lowered her voice. "I have over one hundred confirmed ISIS kills. How many bad guys have you killed?"

No way. She was pulling his leg. He knew several SEALs who had double-digit confirmed kills, and everyone in the world knew Chris Kyle had over 160 confirmed kills, but Hannah? The small-framed woman sitting across the table from him didn't look like the cool warrior persona of a sniper. She looked like the daughter of American doctors who enjoyed a good life of skiing at high-end resorts.

He didn't know whether to believe her or not. One thing was sure, he'd know how well she shot soon enough.

Hannah had insisted they stop by the house so she could pick up her weapons. Isaac got his own and checked in with Guardian Security. Her family was safe; their personal protection was checking in every four hours. The operations center hadn't noticed any unusual activity around the slope-side house. Feeling confident, they headed toward the training course for the Winter Olympics biathlon.

Luckily, they were the only car in the parking lot.

After the third shooting station, Isaac was beginning to believe Hannah had told him the truth. The woman could shoot. No matter the position, her bullets hit bullseyes. Some snipers he'd known shut out the whole world around them and focused only on the target in the crosshairs. Hannah seemed extremely aware of everything around her as she took aim and released bullets downrange.

The woman was fucking amazing.

Isaac was no sniper, but he had always shot expert. He'd practically been raised with a gun in his hand. His father had taken him hunting since he was old enough to walk. He'd spent hours shooting soda cans off fence posts with the .22 his father had given him for his eighth birthday. A pang of sadness bounced off his heart. That had been the year his mother had died. Two years later, his father didn't have time for him anymore. He'd been too busy trying to keep his new wife happy.

"Isaac, you're up." Hannah's voice broke through the rough path down memory lane. Thank God.

He kneeled and positioned the rifle to his shoulder. He wasn't using the .22 long rifle the competition mandated, but instead, he had chosen his M4 a wounded veteran had built for him. Checking the slight wind, he moved the crosshairs a fraction to the left.

Bam.

He'd shot just to the left of center on the first of the five targets. He was dead center by the fifth.

55

Glancing over at Hannah's, her first one was a little tiny bit high and to the right, but each one after that was perfect.

Instead of his normal competitive streak rearing its ugly head, Isaac was proud of her. He wanted to go over and sling his arm around her shoulders and tell her how pleased he was, honored even to be shooting was someone of her caliber.

Instead, he simply told her, "Good job." He stood. "It's about a kilometer to the next one." *Good job. That's the kind of thing you say to your dog.* He certainly wasn't scoring any points with her. But, in truth, he didn't need to score points with Hannah. This wasn't a date, and she wasn't his girlfriend, nor could she ever be. This was work. She was the job. He was simply testing the skills of the woman in the stretchy pants that hugged that perfect ass and those long powerful legs.

Isaac slung his gun onto his back and stretched his stride to catch up with Hannah who was already twenty feet in front. He glanced around the shooting area, relatively sure they hadn't been followed at all that day. They'd been making decisions spontaneously so it wasn't as though anyone could get ahead of them and set up an ambush.

After hours of fighting temperatures in the low twenties, pushing their bodies to stay vertical while skiing downhill, then competing in their own mini-biathlon, Isaac was ready to call it a day. Hannah had performed far beyond his expectations. She was incredible. Strong. Focused. Yet pleasantly feminine. He had no doubt she would be able to handle a few hours of backcountry tomorrow.

Taking out his phone, Isaac suggested, "Let's get some burgers and fries to go. Would you be okay with watching a movie tonight?"

Hannah yawned. "That sounds absolutely perfect. I don't feel like dealing with people right now." She leaned on her polls and gazed up at the surrounding mountain peaks. "I love it out here. It's so beautiful and quiet."

She held Isaac's gaze. "Thank you for bringing me here. I was fine as long as it was just you and me on the slopes." She shuddered. "But when we got down to the lodge, I got too anxious. There were way too many people. I didn't like the way it made me feel."

Neither did Isaac. Alone on the biathlon course with Hannah made for a perfect afternoon. He called a small grill located in the village and placed their order. It was a few blocks out of the way, but worth the trip according to his local friends. They weren't wrong.

He and Hannah had entered the house through the lower-level equipment room and put their gear away, wiping everything dry before properly stowing it. In silence, they had wolfed down the burgers at the dining table before Hannah announced she was taking a shower.

Isaac took the opportunity to call the Operations Center at his office. "Anything to report?"

"We had a year-old dark green Jeep Cherokee make three passes very slowly," the technician on duty reported concisely. "We ran the plates and they checked out okay. It's a rental from the Bozeman airport. A couple of men from Chicago hitting the slopes for a few days."

"Contact me if they cruise by again."

"Will do. Ops Center out."

Erring on the safe side, Isaac rechecked every door and every window.

When Hannah emerged from the master bedroom, long wet strands of hair dripped onto the silky tank top she wore over nothing but magnificent breasts. The water had made the material nearly see-through as it clung to her dark nipples.

His mouth went dry as he tried to swallow.

He hoped the baggie ski pants hid his erection that grew and hardened with every step she took toward him. Thank goodness she hadn't even looked up to see him standing at the end of the hallway.

He wasn't sure he'd ever known such a beautiful woman.

The fact that he liked her, respected her, made his attraction even worse.

Of their own volition, his legs started to move toward her.

She abruptly turned and stepped into the small

bathroom in the hall. His bathroom. Where his shaving kit sat open on the granite counter. Where Karl, his best friend from the Atlanta Center, had tossed in a box of condoms while he packed for Montana. *What if she sees them?*

So what? He was a twenty-six-year-old healthy male…who hadn't had sex in over a year. But she didn't need to know that.

He reached the door about the same time she did.

"Sorry." She held up a hair dryer. "I needed this."

The scent of coconut hit him like a sledgehammer. She smelled good enough to eat. At that moment, he felt as though he could devour every inch of Hannah, starting at her neck and ending between her legs.

She looked up at him with a self-deprecating smile that made him want to lean down and kiss her.

He couldn't do that. He was there to protect her, not to make her come around his tongue, then again around his cock. Although having her in his bed would be the ultimate way of keeping her close, she was also a distraction. He couldn't keep her safe if his brain was more focused on sliding into her wet, moist heat than external threats.

He shoved his hands in his pockets so he wouldn't reach up and touch her.

"I need to take a shower." And take care of the insistent bulge in his pants. "The operations center is watching the outside and will call me if they see

KALYN COOPER

anything suspicious." Atlanta also had eyes on the inside of the house, a fact he didn't dare forget.

"Okay." She turned and walked back toward the master bedroom.

Isaac stared as her tight butt cheeks rose and fell. He wanted to grasp them, one in each hand, feeling them tighten and release as she rode his cock, taking them both to a place no bodyguard and client should ever go.

Stepping into the bathroom, he turned on the water and stripped. With the heat washing over him, he moaned his release for the first time in a year. He wasn't sure whether to rejoice knowing his dick still worked or chastise himself for wanting a woman he couldn't have.

A knock on the door preceded her muffled voice. "Since you lost the biathlon, I'm picking the movie."

"Go right ahead." He'd sit through a chick flick if it meant being near her.

CHAPTER 6

HANNAH HADN'T MISSED ISAAC'S IMPRESSIVE HARD-ON when she'd gone to get the hairdryer. It wasn't until she looked in the mirror in the master bathroom that she realized she looked like a candidate in a wet T-shirt contest.

She was thrilled he liked her body. She worked hard to stay in shape. Until last week, she ran at least five miles every morning, lifted weights for an hour, and spent at least two hours every other day at one of the ranges. Someday, hopefully soon, she would return to Syria and her position with the YPJ. There was so much left to do, and she had the skills to make a difference.

Maybe that's where she should have gone rather than hide in the United States. She hated that her parents had been hurt because of her.

Or maybe she should just go hunting here in the

USA. She had a talent for finding the radicals. The perfect shot from half a mile away would be easy and give her plenty of opportunities to escape. But over there she had more assistance. In Syria, she was a hero. In the USA, she'd be a murderer.

No. She would allow Homeland Security to find the terrorist cells and eliminate them. Then her family could live in peace, and she would return to the Middle East.

Sitting on the floor, she flipped through drawer after drawer of DVDs. Nothing seemed to appeal. The television was on a national headline news program currently discussing the weather.

"Want something to drink?" Isaac headed toward the kitchen in soft, knee-length shorts and a faded Go Navy T-shirt that hugged every one of his delectable muscles. Damn, he was cut.

"No, thank you. I'm good." From the corner of her eye, Hannah watched the muscles in his arm roll and flex as he grabbed a sports drink. Waking up surrounded by those arms would make any woman feel safe. She'd been on the run for weeks. Living on the edge drained a person. To let it all go, just for one night, allow someone else to take care of her, would be a dream come true.

Hannah glanced up as Isaac set his gun down on the table next to the couch. Yes, he might be just what she needed. He looked completely capable of fulfilling her needs. If his earlier physical reaction to her was any indication, she might even get an orgasm out of it. That would make it even nicer.

She couldn't remember when she'd last experienced the big O. Aziz had shown up in their forward camp only a few times in her final months in Syria. Their sex had been *wham, bam, thank you, ma'am.* He'd been more interested in their pillow talk afterward than seeing to her needs. And she'd let him get away with it rather than demanding her own release.

She had been such an idiot to believe his lies. Now he was dead, and she was on the run from his vengeful family.

"Looks like that snowstorm is finally moving in," Isaac noted as he settled onto the couch and kicked sock-covered feet onto the coffee table. "I'm glad we got in a whole day of skiing, though."

"Me, too." She had thoroughly enjoyed the day. "If it snows, are we still going—"

"...al Hasakah—"

Hannah's head popped up at the news announcer's mention of the small town in Northwestern Syria close to ISIS claimed territories.

"...twenty-five girls ages eight to fourteen were kidnapped and the four nuns running the remote school were killed."

Hannah leaped to her feet and stared at the television in horror as pictures of smiling children in makeshift classrooms typical of that area flashed across the screen. Her heart started to beat faster and faster as she sipped shallow breaths. She had been to that school. She'd spoken with the nuns.

"No. No. No!" She cried out. "The YPJ vowed to protect them. Where the hell was my all-female battalion? How could they have let this happen?" This was her fault. She had made promises to the nuns and wasn't there to keep the girls safe.

Video scanned the charred remains of the once-thriving school. The camera zoomed in on a still-burning book as the newscaster announced that ISIS had taken credit for the devastation.

"We brought them those books when the physicians came to immunize the girls." She and twenty-five of her best warrior women had escorted a group from Doctors Without Borders to several isolated schools. They had also transported dozens of books, colorful modern clothing, and feminine necessities for the girls coming of age.

Abu Bakr al-Baghdadi, the leader of ISIS and Aziz's brother, spoke in Arabic about how his soldiers had freed the easily-influenced young women from the clutches of a modern world and he would personally oversee their proper Islamic education. The English translation printed on the bottom of the screen didn't get it quite correct. His word choice was considerably more exploitative.

"Yeah, right." Hannah sneered. "Their virginity was your gift to the soldiers who will make them slaves. Their so-called proper education will be in ways to make a man come in every orifice of their tiny bodies. If they fight back, they will be beaten to within an inch of their life." Hannah gasped, trying to force air into her lungs. That was when she realized she was crying. She had seen the brutality inflicted by his men. She had personally freed more than three dozen of the helpless girls militants had turned into sex slaves.

She had to go there.

Now.

Hannah spun toward her bedroom and sprinted down the hall.

"Are you all right?" Isaac called as he followed her.

Hannah grabbed her travel bag from under the bed and started stuffing clothes into it. If she were moving back to Syria, she would need more than the mere essentials she carried in her grab-n-go bag.

"Where do you think you're going?" he asked.

"Back to Syria." She opened her underwear drawer and scooped everything into her arms, carrying the load to the duffel on her bed. She dumped it in the bag and turned to retrieve more clothes.

Isaac grabbed her wrists. "You're not going anywhere."

She looked at him through tear-filled eyes. "I have to." She sniffed. "Did you see what those fuckers did? I promised the nuns they would be protected." Tears streamed down her face. Pointing toward the living room she screamed, "Those little girls are now in the clutches of savages because I wasn't there to protect them."

Hannah shook her hands loose from Isaac's grasp, returning to her dresser for jeans.

Isaac punched his fists on his hips and shook his head. "How do you know this isn't a ploy to make you move? The minute you hop on an airplane, they would find you...and kidnap you. They would haul you back to their desert base and force you to suffer the same fate as those young girls." Through clenched teeth, he added, "Or even worse, they would decide you're not worth it and just kill you."

He pulled her to his broad chest and ran a soothing hand up and down her back. "I can't let that happen."

Helplessness overtook her. She wrapped her arms around his waist and let her head drop to his shoulder. For the first time in years, she allowed the tears to flow rather than turn them into anger and determination. Those young girls were more than six thousand miles away, and she could do nothing to stop the brutality that had started the moment they were taken. Without a doubt, the YPJ was already looking for their location, planning a raid and rescue.

Hannah allowed that knowledge, and the faith in the women she had trained beside, to help her regain her composure. She replaced the horrific pictures on television with memories of looking down her scope, an ISIS soldier in the crosshairs. Her battalion would find those young girls and free them.

To get her unruly emotions under control, Hannah dragged in a deep breath and inhaled the distinct scent of man. It was intoxicating. She could easily escape into his comfort, allowing his arms to shield her from the evil of the world. How she longed to fall deep asleep next to this man.

She rolled her head and laid her lips on his neck.

His breathing caught for one heartbeat, then he released it slowly. She wasn't sure what his reaction meant, so she kissed her way around his beard to the spot just below his ear.

Pressed up against him, chest to chest, hips to hips, thigh to thigh, she mentally fist-pumped back the way his cock leaped to life.

Oh, yes. He wanted her. For just one night, she could take what she needed from this very willing man.

She smiled and sucked the lobe of his ear into her mouth.

Isaac's hands flew to her shoulders, and he took a giant step backward, nearly out into the hallway. "Hannah, you're upset." He dropped his hands and then shoved them in his pockets. "I never should've touched you. I'm sorry."

"I'm not." Grinning, she closed the distance between them. "And I liked the way you touched me." She ran her hands up his solid chest and wove them around his neck. "Do it again," she whispered as she traced her tongue over the curves of his ear.

His chest shuddered as he let out a long breath. She could feel his hands, still buried in his pockets, ball into fists. "Hannah, we can't do this." He glanced up into the corner of the hallway and for the first time, she noticed a small red light.

Was that a camera? She thought it was just a motion detector. Angry, she dropped her arms, placing her hands on her hips. "Is there video surveillance *in* the house?"

Isaac looked at his stocking feet and quietly answered, "Yes. And audio."

She glanced over her shoulder to her bedroom. "Everywhere?"

He looked at her and quickly reassured her, "No. Hallways, all the main areas, stairwells. The outdoor cameras cover every exit and window."

"Is someone watching us all the time?" Her mind raced back through the past several days. She never made a habit of walking around naked, but there might've been times before Isaac arrived that she had walked down the hall in a lacy bra and matching bikini panties.

"Hannah, you are a high-value target," he said as though that explained everything.

"Have these always been video and audio?" She knew her voice was accusing but couldn't stop it.

"Yes." Isaac then shook his head. "No. When the

system was installed it had full capabilities, but since the house wasn't used very often, the local security company left them on motion sensors. I converted it when I arrived and changed everything over to our Guardian Security system."

Whew. That was a relief. Then she remembered her wet shirt and very visible dark nipples. She shrugged. What was done was done. She couldn't change the past. "Well, I hope they enjoyed my show the other night."

The corners of Isaac's mouth kicked up. "I certainly did," he said just above a whisper barely moving his lips.

She stepped back into the depths of her bedroom, hoping he would follow her into her personal privacy. He stopped at the doorway, his hands braced on either side.

She spun around and looked into his deep brown eyes. "Are the cameras why you won't touch me?"

His chin dropped to his chest. "No." He raised his head slowly. His gaze felt like fingers touching every part of her body as he visually traced her curves from her ankles to her teasing smile. "You know how much I want you." He glanced down at his tented shorts. "I can't hide that fact. But I'm here to protect you. If I'm concentrating on licking and sucking your clit until you scream my name, or thrusting inside you seeking my own release, I'm not focused on the next threat."

Dirty talk had never excited Hannah before, but now she tingled at her core and went wet at the vision he painted. She could practically feel the heat of his breath on her thighs. Oh, yes. She wanted that. Now would be nice.

Like the burst of frigid air when a door opens in the wintertime, she realized the rest of his words. If they were wrapped up in sex, they were both vulnerable. Literally exposed. More than once, she'd shot a target with his pants down.

He was right, damn it.

Suddenly tired, the letdown after an adrenaline rush, she announced, "I'm going to bed." She looked up at the gorgeous man who filled her doorway. "Unfortunately, alone."

"I'll check the house before calling it a night." Isaac turned and walked away.

Hannah tossed the half-packed duffel onto the floor and crawled into bed. After her day of exertion, sunshine, and fresh air, exhaustion quickly overtook her.

"Hannah." Isaac's voice pulled her from a deep sleep. Still in a sleep fog, she couldn't comprehend the words, but his tone was clear. Before she could roll out of bed, he was standing on one leg in the doorway, sliding the other into long underwear.

"We're leaving right now. Plan to be in the cold for several hours." Isaac's rushed words shot ice into Hannah's veins.

CHAPTER 7

Isaac's phone had buzzed on the nightstand what seemed like five minutes after he'd fallen asleep. Opening his eyes, he checked the clock. It was four-thirty in the morning. He lifted the phone and adrenaline shot straight to his heart when he saw the caller ID was Guardian's Atlanta Operations Center.

Before he could utter a word, the man on the other end urgently said, "Get her out of there. Now."

Phone in hand, Isaac grabbed the long underwear he knew he would need and hurried to Hannah's open door, calling her name. Her eyes blinked several times as she focused on him. He barked out urgent orders which she seemed to accept, leaving the bed and quickly dressing warmly.

Turning back to his own room, Isaac demanded, "Sit rep." Secretly he hoped the situational report was not as bad as he had feared.

He was wrong.

"Satellite surveillance shows two heat signatures sitting in an SUV five hundred feet down the street." That wasn't good news, but the man back in Atlanta didn't stop there. "Second SUV with two people in the front seats located one hundred fifty feet to the east. Two tangos approaching very slowly from the back."

"Fuck." Isaac slid into his cold-weather clothes. Since he never unpacked, he grabbed his bag in his free hand and headed across the hall, hoping Hannah had at least found some clothes to wear. He'd dress her himself if he had to.

"Confirming, your count is six tangos."

"Count is correct," the ops center attendant replied.

Hannah stepped into the hall at the same time he did. She was dressed all in white with a ski mask covering her gorgeous long, dark hair. She held a pistol in her right hand, a large duffel in her left, and had a sniper rifle slung down her back.

Who the fuck was this woman? He had never known a female to get ready so fast, but he'd never known one whose life depended on dressing in seconds.

Six? She mouthed.

He nodded.

She went to the natural wood fireplace and

grabbed some ashes, smearing her pristine clothes with shades of gray and black.

Camouflage. A damn good idea. Isaac looked at his black pants and black turtleneck. He selected white ashes and started making splotches all over his clothes.

"My SUV is parked a block away, out the back," Hannah handed Isaac the burned end of a log and turned her back to him.

"We'll have to get past the two guys in the back-yard." Not needing further instruction, he made squiggly lines and broad swaths of black, breaking up the white of her outline.

"No problem, as long as you can quietly take out your guy." Hannah turned around to face him for a second then shoved his shoulders so she could apply white dust to his back.

She smacked his ass. "You're good to go."

Moving like a ball in a pinball game, darting around the dark living room, he watched Hannah collect weapons from the couch, stuffed down the sides of chairs, strapped underneath the dining table, and behind the kickboard under kitchen cabinets.

Holy hell. She'd been prepared for an all-out attack. Thank God. Most of his larger weapons were still in the back of his SUV.

"When were you going to tell me about all that?" Isaac asked as she strode toward him. "Your arsenal would've been good to know about earlier, too."

She walked past him and headed toward the stairs to the basement. "I didn't know if I could trust you. I thought I might need to use them against you."

Isaac wanted to grin. "So, you trust me now?"

"Looks like it," was her only confirmation as she disappeared down the stairwell.

They kept to the shadows on the far side of the recreation room, away from the moonlight shining through the sliding glass doors that led to the backyard. Isaac about had a heart attack when Hannah stopped in the small downstairs kitchen. She opened the freezer and pulled out yet another gun and two magazines.

She reached underneath the breakfast counter. "How are you fixed for weapons?" She pulled out an Uzi mini submachine gun. "Do you want to take this one?"

"Never turn down a weapon," the senior chief had once said during tactical training. Reaching for it, Isaac checked the chamber. Of course, it was loaded. He made sure the safety was on and shoved it into the side pocket of his bag.

In the equipment room, they grabbed their backcountry packs. Isaac was thankful he listened to the little voice in his head when he also brought in his boots and telemark skis the night before. He'd wanted to check the fit of the new skins and give them one more coat of wax.

On his knees, he reached into the small bag he'd

brought from Guardian Security and pulled out two small boxes. "This is for you."

Hannah glanced over her shoulder at the small dark case in his hand. "I hope that's a communications unit and not an engagement ring."

He was glad she used humor to relieve the stress of the situation. His SEAL team often exchanged crude jokes just before stepping into danger.

The heavily padded container was about the same size as a ring box. This time, Isaac didn't hold back a smile as he slid the tiny device into his ear and informed the ops center technician that he was switching from telephone to field communications.

While Atlanta couldn't hear, he leaned in close to her. "I couldn't marry a woman I hadn't even fucked yet...or at least tasted."

He watched Hannah's huge brown eyes turn to molten milk chocolate in the small penlight they were using in the closed room. His boss would not be happy with his rough language around a client, but Isaac liked teasing her.

Refocusing, Isaac tapped his ear. "Atlanta Center, comm check."

"Loud and clear," came the reply. "Code name for this op?"

"Designate Snowman." He'd been tagged with the name when he first started BUD/S, the schooling every SEAL must complete. It had stuck.

Hannah's smile lit up the room, or at least his

heart. "I like it. It's appropriate." She flicked the tiny button to activate her device. After embedding it in her ear. "Testing. This is Hannah Kader, code name Blink."

"Blink?" That was one of the strangest handles Isaac had ever heard.

She gave him a shit-eating grin. "Yeah, piss me off, and I'll kill you in the blink of an eye."

She slid into the backpack straps and buckled them securely around her hips and across her chest. She handed him her alpine touring skis. "Tuck these into the straps, please."

"Tango one is thirty feet down the hedge on the east side of the yard." The clarity of the transmission from Atlanta was amazing. "He just slipped over to the neighbor's side to avoid the automatic external lights. No worries for you. I have disabled them."

"What happened to tango two?" Isaac held Hannah's gaze.

"He's playing peeping Tom at the house next door which we already know is vacant," Atlanta informed them.

"Should I take him out?" Hannah looked at Isaac as she asked the question, but she could have been asking Atlanta for sanction on the kill.

"Let's keep this extraction as clean as possible."

Isaac stilled at the sound of Alex Wolf's voice. *The owner of the company*, he mouthed to Hannah who nodded in understanding.

"SOCOM and Homeland are watching with us, but no one has assets close enough to help you tonight." Alex's voice sounded regretful.

That explained why they had thermal satellite in real-time. This was so much bigger than Isaac had ever imagined when he agreed to take this personal protection gig. With the two government agencies on board, he didn't dare fuck up protocol. No matter what, though, he had to get Hannah to safety.

He withdrew the six-inch, black matte blade from the sheath on his belt. Its rough handle was comfortable against his palm. It had killed before and would do so at least once more.

"You stay here until I give you the all-clear," Isaac ordered Hannah.

"Not fucking likely." Hannah screwed the silencer onto her pistol. "You need backup."

"Listen to the lady," Alex instructed. "Never underestimate a woman warrior."

"Yes, sir." Isaac then added, "That sounds like the voice of experience."

Low male laughter rumbled through his earpiece. "You haven't met the other owner of Guardian Security, Katlin Callahan, have you?"

"No, sir. I haven't had the privilege," Isaac admitted.

"When this is over, I'll make that happen," Alex promised.

"Atlanta Center here. Suggest you move now.

Tango one is twenty feet from your location. Tango two is returning to the backyard."

Isaac took one last look at Hannah. Her single nod was all the consent he needed. "Moving out."

In step, knees bent, Hannah's hand on his shoulder, they slipped silently down the hedge in the deepest of shadows.

Two yards in front of them, the bushes shook.

"He's decided to cut through to your side," Atlanta announced.

"Permission granted." There was no hesitation in Alex's voice.

Isaac was waiting as the man dressed in nighttime camouflage stepped through the evergreen bushes. Grabbing his head, Isaac spun him around and cut his throat.

But not before the tango had a chance to grunt out a warning.

Isaac shoved Hannah down, her back to the ground, as a bright light flashed across the yard a millisecond before a loud blast. Tango two had shot at them.

Hannah pushed Isaac off her and leaned up.

Phew. Phew.

They didn't bother watching the second tango fall. They were already on their feet running toward the back of the yard and the street beyond.

"All four tangos are out of the vehicles and in

pursuit," the Atlanta tech calmly relayed. "Slide through the bushes on your right."

Isaac grabbed Hannah's hand and pulled her through the prickly holly hedge without losing stride. Staying close to the large trees to minimize their footprints, they sprinted toward the back of a house and then around the side.

"Down there." Hannah pointed to a white SUV and the vehicle started.

He heard the locks release. "Gotta love modern technology." Isaac headed toward the driver's door. "Give me the keys."

"I've got this." Hannah shoved him toward the other side. "You just be prepared to shoot if they decide to follow us." She flung open the front door and threw her bag on the center console then jogged to the back, clumsily shucking off her backpack. Skis that were as long as her body made handling the heavy backpack awkward. Isaac didn't have near as much problem and shoved hers in on top of his before quietly closing the hatch. No need to advertise their location.

"Where are those tangos?" Isaac asked in a hushed voice.

"They're spreading out. Closest one is fifteen hundred feet. He's tracking you down the treeline." Thankful Guardian Security had his back, Isaac was even more grateful for Alex's connections at the highest levels. At that moment, they had their own satellite.

As he slid onto the passenger seat, Hannah was pulling on her safety belt. "I've been told they train SEALs to steady a shot while standing on a boat in the middle of a rolling ocean. I hope you can apply those skills to a moving vehicle." She opened the roof.

"Brings all new meaning to riding shotgun," Isaac said as he dug his M4 out of his duffel before shoving the bag into the back seat.

Hannah took off like a bat out of hell. "Where am I going?"

"To the base of the slopes. Turn right at the next corner." Isaac hoped someone he knew was working that night.

"What's your plan, Snowman?" Alex asked.

"I'm going to try to hitch a ride on a snow cat to the top of the mountain," Isaac explained. "They should be grooming the slopes by now. We'll hide out until sunrise then we'll backcountry ski to a cabin I know on the east side of Lone Mountain."

"Coordinates?" the Atlanta tech asked.

"Unknown." Although Isaac had been to Uncle Samuel's cabin multiple times, he had never needed a compass or GPS. "I'll ping the location when we arrive."

"I'm not seeing a cabin or a road anywhere on that side of the mountain." The operations center technician sounded slightly aggravated.

Isaac chuckled. "And you won't. There is no road, and the cabin is hidden under pine trees that stand a hundred feet tall. Once we build the fire, you might be able to see the heat signature. By the way, where are the tangos?"

"Wandering through backyards of very expensive homes, setting off motion sensors everywhere." He could hear the amusement in Alex's voice. "The local police have been notified of a group of burglars in the area and are already responding."

Hannah parked under a light in the nearly vacant parking lot. "Should I be worried about the SUV?"

"No," Isaac answered at the same time as several other men.

"Homeland Security has a team heading your way from Billings," Alex informed them. "They'll handle returning your vehicle and hopefully take the men chasing you into federal custody."

"Will I be safe then?" Hannah asked as she grabbed her bag. Isaac helped her into her backpack, readjusting her skis so they rode more comfortably.

"I'm afraid not, Blink." Alex went on to reassure her, "But SOCOM has a few things in the works and hopefully you can return to your family soon."

"In the meantime, we're headed to the safest place I know." Isaac's gaze swept the parking lot one last time before he closed the tall wooden fence gate at the employee entrance to what employees fondly called the Cat House.

"Have you ever hitchhiked before?" Isaac asked as he led her to the maintenance building.

CHAPTER 8

HANNAH'S THIGHS BURNED, HER CALVES ACHED, AND she was positive she had used muscles that had never been stretched and pulled before. When Isaac had said the cabin was on the backside of Lone Mountain, he had neglected to say there was a mini-mountain in between.

Fortunately, they had gained enough speed to make it part way up but climbing at seven thousand feet above sea level with six-foot boards strapped to her feet was far from a walk on the paved part of the Atlanta BeltLine. Then there was the added weight of her pack and her duffel which Isaac had cleverly strapped into one unit. It weighed as much as she did, but she had kept up without a single complaint.

Isaac had been right. The cabin was so remote she immediately felt safe.

"We'll leave our skis out here," he said as he leaned his against the bare logs under the porch.

"Talk about the convenience of skiing in and out, this place is perfect." Hannah jammed the tip of her pole into her binding, releasing the boot.

"It doesn't get near as much snow here under the canopy," Isaac explained. "The pine trees act like an umbrella. They also protect this place from the wind."

"But aren't those steps?" She pointed to where the railings left a six-foot opening and placed her skis next to his.

Isaac's smile warmed her all the way through. "Yeah. There's about four feet of snow out there. That's nothing compared to the seventy-five inches at the top of the mountain."

Isaac walked to the far end of the porch and ran his hands underneath one of the protruding log ends. It popped open to reveal a security pad and keys. He entered a code and she heard metal scraping on metal.

"Steel rods secure the door," he explained, returning the wood piece. "Uncle Samuel is a bit of a security nut."

"I'll thank him for that as soon as I get to meet him."

Isaac gave her an incredulous look. "What makes you think you're going to meet that old goat?"

"Doesn't he live here?" she asked as he pushed the door open.

"No." Isaac stepped aside to make room for her on the commercial-grade rug. "He has a house just outside Bozeman. I would never call this a hunting cabin because that would assume he comes here to primarily hunt. It's more like his autonomous zone." He smiled. "My uncle doesn't like people, so he hides away from the rest of the world here. Although during the season, he also uses this as a base camp for hunting."

Hannah wasn't sure what she had expected, but this wasn't even close. Although it lacked feminine touches, it had every modern amenity. Two recliners, separated by an end table, could be swiveled to face the large screen television that took up most of one wall or turned toward the huge stone fireplace in the center of the open concept room. A six-person dining table sat on the far side. A long breakfast island separated the kitchen, which gleamed with stainless steel appliances.

She felt Isaac tug on her pack and allowed him to hold it while she slid out of the straps. She turned to help him, but his pack already sat on the floor.

He kneeled and reached in, extracting his snow boots. "I need to get the generator started. Take the bedroom on the left. There should be clean sheets in the hall closet."

"Thanks." She smiled sheepishly. "Does this place have running water? I...um...need—"

"Give me two minutes to get the generator running. It provides power to the pump." He grinned. "Or you're welcome to pick a tree. They're so big around here, I'd never see you hiding behind one."

"No worries, Snowman, it wouldn't be the first time I peed outdoors." A memory suddenly crossed her mind. "Remember the trees we hit at the base of Lone Mountain? The last time my brother and I went backcountry, the guide had us build camp about fifty yards into those woods. I can guarantee you; I marked the base of several trees in that area."

"First, no need for codenames anymore." His white smile blended with the frozen snow embedded in his beard. "As soon as we got here, I pinged the location and Atlanta dropped all communication. When the generator is up, I'll turn on the external sensors and connect them to Guardian. Second, that's a great place to camp. Third, we have a complete bathroom here and hot water. Or we will have hot water as—"

She giggled and they completed the sentence together. "As soon as you get the generator going."

He was so easy to be around, fun even. He truly seemed to enjoy teasing her.

"I called you Snowman because you look like one, right now." With her index finger, she touched his cold, bluish lips, tracing their outline. "Even your lips are nearly white."

He bent to her ear and just above a whisper, he asked, "Care to warm them up for me? There are no cameras or audio equipment inside this cabin."

"Good to know." She leaned back and brushed her lips across his. "There's more where that came from, but first, I'm freezing my ass off. You get that generator started, and I'll build a fire." She turned toward the wood stacked conveniently next to the large stone fireplace.

He grabbed her arm and she spun on the heels of the stiff ski boots, stopping only when she smacked into his chest. "I know a lot of ways to warm up that pretty little ass of yours."

Then he crashed his mouth on hers. The heat of his tongue as he slipped it into her mouth was such a contrast with the ice of his beard pressing against her face. His kiss was hot and demanding as his arms wrapped around her body. His large hand dropped to her derrière as he gently ran his fingers over her cheeks, then cupped them, pulling her into his erection.

She wasn't sure who pulled away first, or if they both needed air at the same time. She lifted her gloved hands to her face. "Before we do that again, you're going to wash the ice out of that beard."

"I'll shave the fucking thing off if that's what it takes to be able to kiss you again." He reached between her legs and cupped her heated mound. "I wouldn't want to leave whisker burn in such a tender spot." He ran the tips of his fingers right up the middle of her sex, setting each nerve on fire.

Hannah wanted to melt right there in a pool of lust. She wasn't sure what had changed Isaac's mind about having sex with her, but she wasn't going to complain. The more she was around him, the more she wanted him deep inside her body.

Isaac stepped back. "I prefer to shave with hot water." He pulled on his boots and left her standing there, wanting him more than she ever wanted any man in her life.

She let out a long slow sigh, hoping it took some of the sexual tension with it. She had a fire to build, beds to make, and a cabin to secure her way. Even though they seemed miles from danger, Aziz's family had found her in Big Sky. They wanted her bad and would not stop until they had captured or killed her.

She took her bags to the bedroom and was surprised at the king-size bed. The headboard and footboard looked handmade, hewn from local trees. She could see herself wrapped around Isaac, snuggling under the green quilt after they'd had hours of satisfying sex.

Knowing death was not only possible but probable, gave Hannah a completely different perspective on life. She was not about to waste one minute more of hers. She wanted Isaac. He wanted her. Without the voyeurs in Atlanta, she couldn't see any reason to stop them.

Just in case they had to leave on a moment's notice again, Hannah decided not to unpack. For years in the Middle East, she'd lived out of bags like the ones that lay at the foot of the bed.

Grabbing several weapons and a roll of duct tape, Hannah returned to the living area. She dispersed handguns and two mini-submachine guns. This time she would tell Isaac exactly where they were located in case he needed them as well. While affixing a pistol to the underside of the cabinet, Hannah heard a vehicle.

Impossible. She had distinctly heard Isaac say there were no roads. At one of their resting stops this morning, he'd explained that everything had been brought in by all-terrain vehicles using different routes each time so as not to create a permanent path.

Gun in hand, Hannah stood in the middle of the room and was pleased to find she could see out in every single direction simply by turning around. She heard the purr of an engine.

Footsteps on the porch drew her attention. She watched Isaac casually walk toward the front door. Only then did she realize the noise she'd heard was the generator, not a vehicle.

Well, damn. She was more on edge than she'd thought. The generators they'd used in the desert coughed and spit, creating so much noise they had to shout if they were anywhere close to one.

Hannah wanted to throw her arms around Isaac the moment he stepped inside, but instead, she returned to hiding the pistol.

"Perimeter is secure, all the motion sensors are working perfectly, the pump is primed, and the propane gas is on," he reported as he took off his jacket and hung it on one of the pegs. He glanced at the fireplace and then at her. "Maybe I need to put this back on until I get a fire going."

She suddenly felt like an idiot. She'd spent the time on security rather than building the fire. "That was next on my list."

"Excellent." Isaac pulled the high-tech sweater over his head and scrunched his nose. "In that case, if you don't mind, I want to take a shower."

"Is the water warm already?" She asked.

"It's an on-demand system," he explained as he padded in his sock feet toward the bedrooms. "Rather than heat up a huge tank of water, the gas heats as you need it."

"So, I can take a shower as long as I want without running out of hot water?" That sounded like heaven to Hannah.

His reply came from down the hall. "Yep. As long as you want."

This could turn out to be better than she'd thought.

Within minutes, Hannah had a beautiful fire started. Her stomach rumbled. After exploring the kitchen cabinets, she discovered hundreds of packages of freeze-dried food and shelves of canned vegetables. Chili had the most appeal and one of the shortest cooking times.

"Something smells good," Isaac noted as he walked out in nothing but a towel wrapped around his waist. "And it's even warm all the way down the hall. Nice fire."

Hannah's gaze was immediately drawn to the white towel. As she forced her eyes upward, she couldn't help but notice the defined V of his hips and the trail of dark hair that led to his belly button. Washboard abs took on a new definition as she counted not three sets but four.

Breathe, her brain demanded. She sucked in a long slow breath as her eyes wandered farther up. He had strong shoulders and distinct pectoral muscles. Continuing her perusal, she noticed for the first time a very square jaw and wide chin.

He had shaved.

The lack of hair had changed everything about his face. The beard had softened the hard planes, but she liked this face.

"Do you want to take a picture? It'll last longer," he teased.

"No need." She dropped her gaze over his body

head to toe, one more time. "This image is burned into my memory and labeled *male perfection*."

"There's more of it to see." He reached for his towel and started to unwrap it. "But maybe I'll wait for the big reveal until after you feed me. To be honest, I'm starved."

"In that case, why don't you go put on some clothes while I dish up the chili," she suggested. She was pretty sure she wouldn't eat anything if she had to look across the table at his naked chest. Although, the idea of smearing chili and licking it off that amazing body did hold some interest.

Twenty minutes and two empty bowls later, Isaac shoved his chair back from the table. "You cooked. I'll clean up while you go shower."

"You trying to tell me I stink?" She smiled as she took her bowl to the sink.

He moved behind her, reaching around to place his dirty dishes next to hers. Her back to his chest, he leaned in and sniffed her neck. "I actually like the smell of female sweat." Then he licked her from her collarbone to her ear. "Mmm. Salty. Shall I see if you taste the same...everywhere?" His big hands came around her, his thumbs skimming the underside of her breasts. Her abdomen shuddered at his light touch.

Hannah knew damn well she'd sweated all day. The early morning adrenaline rush of being chased by religious radicals, followed by hours of downhill, cross-country, and uphill skiing in bright sunshine made her thankful for the wick away, high-tech clothing she wore.

If she were going to sleep with this man, she'd do it with a clean body. His hands moved up to cup her breasts. Her nipples hardened. When he rolled them between his thumb and forefinger, she went wet.

"I have a better idea." She rubbed her ass against his erection. "Why don't we take a shower together?"

He bent down and scooped her up, lifting her off the floor into his arms. "I like the way you think."

He carried her into the only bathroom in the house. "I'll be right back. Be naked."

Hannah wasn't sure she liked being bossed around. She was an independent woman, an officer in the Syrian army. She gave orders. But she needed the shower. She could just as easily close and lock the door, although she was pretty sure that wouldn't keep Isaac from coming in anyway. She started peeling off clothes and tossed them into a corner hoping there was a washer and dryer somewhere.

Isaac reappeared, gloriously naked with a foil packet in his hand. He stopped in the doorway and watched her peel off her long underwear. Her white bra and cotton panties were utilitarian, not sexy at all, but she couldn't tell that by the heat in his eyes. She reached around the back to unhook her bra.

In one long step, he stood in front of her. "No, let me do that." He wrapped one hand around her back and with the slide of his fingers, the two hooks released. His hands on her shoulders were so gentle as he slid the straps down her arms and tossed the bra aside.

He stared at her small breasts for what seemed like an eternity.

"They're perfect," he said just above a whisper. He lowered his head and licked his way around her areola. "Not quite as salty." Then he sucked her breast deep into his mouth.

Hannah didn't bother to hold in the moan. Her breasts were very sensitive and seemed to be connected directly to her clit. Surprised it was possible, she became even wetter.

He released her breast and blew cool air over her already puckered nipple before he switched to the other side. This was such sweet torture.

Running his tongue between her breasts, over her quivering abdomen to her belly button, he kneeled in front of her.

In a sensation like she'd never had before, he ran his tongue along the top edge of her panties. Back in college, she would've been embarrassed for not wearing one of her many pairs of lacy panties or a sexy thong. But after a week in the desert, she had thrown them all away and replaced them with sturdy cotton.

"Isaac," she managed to gasp out just before he hooked his thumbs in the sides and drew them down her legs. She stepped out and kicked them aside. Once again he was staring at her, but this time at the neatly trimmed hair that covered her sex.

Aziz had thought it disgusting that she had shaved all but a small swath. He had insisted she let it grow back naturally. She, accustomed to U.S. grooming standards, continued to at least keep it trimmed neatly. She didn't want to think about her former lover with Isaac on his knees in front of her. She wanted—no, needed—him to replace all the memories of the traitor.

She cupped Isaac's face in her hands and forced him to look up at her. "Shower. Now."

When he started to protest, she pulled on his head, forcing him to stand.

"You are so beautiful," he said and tenderly kissed her. When he pulled back, her eyes met his and saw questions. "Hannah, are you sure you want to do this?"

She reached down and grabbed his cock, giving it a slight squeeze. "More than you will ever know."

CHAPTER 9

Isaac reached over and turned on the water. It was going to be a tight squeeze even though he and Uncle Samuel had built the shower for men their size.

Hannah was obviously uncomfortable with him going down on her. Not a problem. Not all women liked oral sex.

They stepped in together, and he allowed the heated water to pelt her shoulders. His had been tight from the uphill trek so he figured hers were, too. When she tilted her head back to let the water soak her hair, exposing that long tan neck of hers, he wanted to kiss his way up it before taking her mouth the way he wanted to take her body. Before he could place the first kiss on her collarbone, she turned to face the showerhead, her back to him.

Well, hell.

He grabbed her shower gel and soaped his hands so he could massage her shoulders. After working up a lather with his hands, he ran them up her neck and over the top of her shoulders. The more he massaged, the more her tension eased. Gliding his soapy hands up her neck and then down over her collarbone, he took both breasts in his hands, gently kneading them. She leaned back against his chest in complete trust.

A space inside him that he hadn't known was empty, suddenly filled. He enjoyed the feel of his fingers sliding all over her soft body. He took his time, starting with her fingertips and working his way up both arms, squeezing and kneading sore muscles. He re-soaped and knelt in front of her.

Kneeling in front of her he picked up one foot and commanded, "Rest it on my thigh."

She did as ordered and he repaid her by smoothing out the muscles with a light grip up and down her calf before moving to her thigh. When he set her foot back down on the tile floor, she automatically raised the other one. He had never given any woman such a sensuous massage. He'd never wanted to before her.

When he reached the juncture of her thighs, he re-soaped, spreading bubbles from hipbone to hipbone. He pressed the heel of his hand over the top of her sex and she shuddered in response.

"I have to taste you," he said through clenched

teeth. He didn't want to push her to do something she wasn't ready for yet, so he asked, "May I?"

"Oh, hell, yes." She cupped her hands on both sides of his face and forced him to look up at her. "Before... I was so sweaty... I didn't want—"

He leaned forward and separated her lips, which were hot and moist from more than just the shower. He ran his hot tongue over her exposed core.

A shudder ran through her whole body.

Hannah was barely breathing. Panting would be the more accurate description. Every muscle in her body had tightened. He knew she was on the edge. She had almost shattered with that single touch.

But that's not the way he wanted their first time to be.

Isaac stood abruptly and turned off the water. "You're going to come around my cock, looking into my eyes, the first time."

Shocked, she just stood there, her almond-shaped eyes almost completely round. He picked her up and carried her to his bed. "I know I'm being selfish, but I want our first time together to be with me deep inside you." Then he smiled. "Maybe the second time I'll have you come around my tongue, or the third." They had days together in the secluded cabin, maybe weeks, without the prying eyes of his office. Only a few people knew their location. She was as safe as she could be, in his arms, in his bed.

He swept back the navy-blue comforter and laid

her on the crisp white sheets, following her down. Ravishing her mouth, his hands found her breasts once again. When he finally reached between her legs, she was soaked. Power and relief washed over him. She wanted him as much as he wanted her.

"Oh, yes." He stroked her once, then twice, before he slid a finger into her wet, hot channel. When he glided in a second digit, he felt her vaginal muscles reflexively clamp around him. "Do that when I'm inside you," he demanded.

He reached for the condom, then remembered he left it in the bathroom. He inwardly smiled. It would get used, probably sooner rather than later. Opening the nightstand drawer, he grabbed another one.

She snatched the packet from his hand. "I want to do that."

He liked the way she was an active participant. His fiancée hadn't been like that at all. She had enjoyed sex—he made sure she came every time and never faked it— but she never took the lead.

Hannah seemed to want to be in control. Not this first time, though.

She tore the package open, tossing the wrapper aside. Her hands were a caress as she rolled the condom down his cock. When she gave him a little squeeze, he slammed his eyes shut to fight for control.

"It was almost over before we got started, sweetheart." As payback, he pumped his fingers in and out of her a few more times before he withdrew them and gently spread her legs farther apart.

When he slid inside her, the word *perfection* popped into his mind. He held himself there for a second and looked down into her blissful face.

"More," she demanded.

His cock swelled at her command.

He backed out slightly then pushed all the way in. This was the way sex was supposed to feel. He filled her completely. She showed her approval as her inner muscles clamped down around him. Hannah was special in a way he couldn't define.

He pumped in and out, but she didn't seem to be getting there. He leaned on one elbow and reached down between them. With the next thrust, he rubbed his thumb over her clit.

Hannah about came off the bed. "Do that again."

Given her reaction, there was no way he would ever deny her.

He leaned down and kissed her quickly. "I'm not going to stop until you scream my name." He then rubbed a circle around the outside of her clitoris and pinched it lightly before he thrust into her.

"I...I.." It sounded as though she tried to call his name, but as he moved inside her, she seemed incapable of speech as she tried to reach higher and higher.

Every muscle in her body tightened. She gasped for breath a second before his name broke on a shuddered exhale. He followed her into a world filled with ecstasy as they both fell over the edge.

ISAAC WAS HAVING the best dream of his life. He and Pete were in Virginia Beach on another bender, celebrating the fact they had both made it out of the sandbox alive once again. They had picked up two women in their favorite oceanside bar, not caring the women were looking to bag a SEAL. Neither man was the kind that would ever settle down and certainly not with a base bunny.

The woman had kissed her way down Isaac's belly and licked the drop of excitement off the tip of his cock. She was currently running her tongue up the very sensitive underside while gently cupping his balls. When she took him in her mouth, he could practically feel her long hair tickle his hips.

Excitement built within him, and he felt ready to burst. He hadn't had a wet dream since he was sixteen. His eyes flew open to find Hannah crouched between his open legs, her head bobbing up and down as she took him deep, all the way to her throat.

"Hannah." Her name was a hoarse plea.

"Huh?" The word was a hum that vibrated through her hot mouth wrapped around his dick.

He clenched his back teeth to fight the urge to come. "Sweetheart, I have a much better idea."

She sat up. "Me, too."

He watched as she rolled on the condom, then straddled his hips before lowering herself onto him. "You don't mind if I go for a ride, do you?"

He reached up and cupped both breasts. "You don't mind if I play with these, do you?" He rolled her nipples between his thumbs and forefingers.

She tightened her thighs on his hips and gave him an internal hug. Oh. Yes. He could get used to this.

They both took a long ride that built slowly. When Isaac was close, he sat up and took her breast in his mouth. He knew the position added pressure to her clit, and she moaned her approval. He wasn't sure how much more he could take so he gently nipped the hardened pebble in his mouth.

Hannah screamed in pleasure. Her internal walls milked every ounce out of him before they collapsed back on the bed.

He didn't want to move, but he had to get rid of the condom. She lay on top of him breathing gently and evenly, asleep in his arms. Perfect.

Carefully, he rolled over to his side and tucked her into the sheets. After disposing the condom and cleaning up, all he wanted to do was go back to her, fall asleep with her for hours, then do it all again.

He heard a buzzing and immediately checked the alarm system. All clear. Then he realized it was the satellite phone that he had placed on vibrate rather than ring. He pressed the button to accept the call as he looked out every window, searching for danger.

"Snowman here."

"Atlanta operations here. You missed your check-in two hours ago. We were about to send in helicopters and our black ops team."

Fuck. Fuck. Fuck! "Sorry. We took showers and fell asleep after finally having a hot meal." When lying, stick as close to the truth as possible. He wondered if they really would send in a team, guns blazing. He was sure he didn't want to find out. "So, now when is my next check-in?"

"Infrared is clear," Atlanta told him. "Go back to bed and take the damn phone with you just in case. Next check-in, oh-six-hundred."

"Snowman out." Isaac clicked off the call. If they had actually been in danger, they would both be dead. He looked down the hall toward his bedroom. The most dynamic, wondrous, vivacious woman he had ever known was waiting for him there. He couldn't let anything happen to her. Ever.

He adjusted the volume to full and crawled in next to Hannah.

His internal alarm woke him at five fifty-five the next morning. The cabin was chilly, so he slipped into sweats and thick socks. He tucked Hannah in and covered her with an extra blanket. Grabbing the sat phone on his way out of the bedroom, Isaac went in search of coffee.

Tonight, he would have to prepare the pot and set the timer so it would be ready when he got up tomorrow. He'd also have to remember to bank the fire so it would last throughout the night.

Coffee dripping, he checked in with Guardian Security.

"There were a few wild animals that wandered by in the night, but none of the two-legged variety. Your uncle has a sweet system. Did you hook him up with that?" Karl Solomon, his best friend back in Atlanta, had the operations center desk that morning.

"What do you think?" was Isaac's reply.

"I think there's a damn good reason that there isn't any surveillance on the inside. I've seen a picture of the pretty lady you're guarding with your life." He lowered his voice. "You had a chance to use that *gift* I sent with you?"

Isaac knew he was talking about the box of condoms. "You know as well as I do, you don't fuck the job." But he had. Several times. And hoped to again this morning.

"You could've gotten a little action before the job actually started." Karl was on a fishing expedition, but Isaac wasn't biting.

"Anything else I need to know about?" He wanted to get off the subject of Hannah. The thought of her warm and soft, and in his bed, made him hard. "Any news from USSOCOM or Homeland?"

"Our former employer is working on something,

but it's top-secret and neither of us has the clearance for that shit anymore." Karl went on to add, "And I, for one, am glad. I've eaten all the sand I'm ever going to, unless I can find some gorgeous woman that needs protecting on a Caribbean beach."

"Roger that." Isaac thought about the plain white bra and panties he had stripped Hannah of last night. It looked like a very conservative bikini. But he didn't have any problems picturing her in three small triangles held together by strings.

His cock was so hard it was pulsing. He looked down the hallway longingly. "Do you have any good news for me?"

"Actually, I do." Then Karl added, "It's really a good news, bad news deal."

"Hit me with the good news first." Isaac poured himself another cup of coffee.

"Homeland has two of the tangos who attacked you in Big Sky in federal custody."

"What about the other two?"

"Sorry, Snowman. Looks like they got away."

Damn. That meant there were at least two men who knew they were in Montana and were close enough to do something about it. Isaac was afraid of that. At least four of the six were out of the game.

"Hang on, Isaac. I have an incoming call from Alex."

When Karl returned to the line, he used his formal voice. "Snowman, hold for Wolf."

The next voice Isaac heard was that of his ultimate boss. "Snowman, are you friendly enough to ask Blink a few questions?"

"Most likely. What do you need to know?" Isaac wasn't sure if Hannah would open up to him.

"We're getting conflicting stories about why ISIS wants her and if they really want her dead, or just want her back." Alex was being vague, and it was driving Isaac's imagination to places he really shouldn't go.

"They want her back so they can torture her?" There was no way in hell Isaac was going to allow that.

There was a long pause before Alex answered. "We have one source telling us that she was the wife of the Caliphate's brother who will take over ISIS if anything happens to al-Baghdadi."

"Holy fuck." The words slipped out of his mouth just above a whisper, but everyone had likely heard them.

"You got that right," Alex confirmed. "If true, that changes everything. You will need to take her into immediate custody so we can turn her over to Homeland Security."

"She could be a fucking spy." The hatred in Karl's voice came through loud and clear.

Isaac quickly thought through everything he and Hannah had spoken about. Had he given away any state secrets?

Of course not.

How could that wonderful woman, the one who had made love to him so tenderly, be an enemy? Isaac shook his head. He couldn't believe what they were saying. It certainly wouldn't be the first time intel was inaccurate.

Married? To someone that high in the fundamentalist regime? No. No way. She was not a woman to hide under an abaya and live as women had a thousand years ago. His Hannah was far too modern to put up with that lifestyle.

When he tuned back in, Alex was talking. "Just see what you can find out and get back to me as soon as possible."

"Yes, sir." Isaac needed answers, too.

CHAPTER 10

"HANNAH, I NEED YOU TO WAKE UP." ISAAC'S VOICE seemed to come from far away. It was not the lover's caress she had expected.

The instant his words penetrated her sleep, Hannah bolted upright. "How close are they?" She threw off the covers and leaped out of bed.

Where the hell are my clothes? Her gaze darted around the unfamiliar room. She tried to put together the pieces of yesterday. Nothing seemed to match up except the fear that had run through her every day and every night since she'd landed in Syria two years ago.

"Where the hell am I?" She heard the panic in her own voice.

Isaac stepped to her and wrapped his arms around her.

She knew him. He equaled safety. When his hand

traced up and down her spine, and he allowed them to just stand there, she knew the danger was not close.

"What's going on?" She leaned back to look into his eyes.

"Why don't you get dressed," he suggested. "Coffee is ready, and I'll whip us up some breakfast." Isaac released her and took a step back.

He didn't seem to be the warm, tender lover from last night. This man was all business. Damn, she hated morning afters. They were always so awkward, but it wasn't like she could get dressed and make the walk of shame back to her own place. She and Isaac were stuck together for the unforeseeable future.

Resigned, she told him, "I'll be there in a minute." Then she reconsidered. "Do I have time for a shower?"

"Sure." Isaac turned and left the room. His one-word sentence told her she was not going to like their next conversation.

Refreshed from a hot shower, dressed in yoga pants that she often wore as long underwear and a turtleneck, Hannah padded in her sock-covered feet into the kitchen, following the smell of food.

From the tight muscles in his face, Isaac looked angry as he stirred cheese into eggs.

Not one to put things off, she jumped right in. "Tell me the bad news."

She watched the muscle in his jaw expand and contract several times.

"Are you married?" He didn't even look at her.

"No." She'd never even been engaged. Although Aziz had often spoken of making her his wife, he had never asked her to marry him. "What gave you that idea?"

Isaac turned the fire off from under the eggs and spun to look at her. "Why does ISIS want you dead?"

Hannah closed her eyes. She knew this day was going to come. She just hated that Isaac was going to be the one to hear her story. He'd realize what an immature child she'd been. She hated to look like a fool, especially to him.

"It's a long story, and one I'm not very proud of." She opened her eyes expecting to see his condemnation already.

His face was totally unreadable.

"Can we at least sit down for this?" She wasn't sure if she could continue to stand.

"Grab the plates," he ordered. "I'm hungry. We'll eat and talk."

She sighed at the reprieve and grabbed two plates from next to the sink where they had dried overnight.

She set her plate on the table, and he took the seat across from her. Shrugging, she admitted, "I'm not sure where to start."

Isaac forked up some eggs and stuffed them in his

mouth. He stared at her as he chewed. He was not going to be any help.

"Okay, you know I was in the YPJ, the all-female battalion in the Syrian army. Since I had three years of college—"

Isaac interrupted her. "Exactly how did you end up in the middle of the civil war in Syria?"

A chuckle escaped before her lips drew into a thin line. "In college, I was studying international relations and political science." A better idea of how to explain it came to her, so she changed directions. "It was just like the other night when we were watching TV. Back then I saw a news flash where young girls in Syria had been kidnapped from a small town near the Iraqi border. It was very close to the refugee camp where I had been born. I felt this tremendous need to go there and help those girls."

His brows drew together. "But you're an American, right?"

"Yes, because my father is a U.S. citizen. He was working in Iraq for the Center for Disease Control when he met my mother who was an ER physician." Unsure if he knew the history of that area, she explained, "Back then, Iraq was actually a progressive country. My brother and sister were both born there too, but they've never claimed dual citizenship."

Isaac got up and grabbed two bottles of water. "Go on." He passed one over to her.

Hannah drank deeply before she set the bottle on

the table. "When things got bad twenty-five years ago, my family fled Iraq in the middle of the night. It took them a few days, but they ended up in a refugee camp in Syria. That's where I was born."

"Got it." Isaac's fork scraped over his empty plate. "Back to my original question, why does ISIS want you so bad?"

"Fast forward to a couple years ago. I left college, flew to Syria, claimed my dual citizenship, and joined the YPG. As I started to tell you, they made me a captain shortly after I had finished my basic training in the Syrian army." She looked down at her plate, still filled with food. This was the stupid part. She inhaled deeply and gathered her fortitude. She couldn't look at the man who had given her such great pleasure the night before as she talked about her former lover. "There was this captain, Aziz al-Habib, who was with the male battalion that usually accompanied us. We...I...I thought we were in love."

She looked up to see how he was going to take the news, but he was feverishly typing into his phone with his thumbs.

What the hell? He's texting?

Here I am bleeding out my soul, and he's fucking texting!

When his eyes finally met hers, he raised one brow. "Tell me more about al-Habib."

"When we first met, he was wonderful. Although his English wasn't great, it was more than passable."

She smiled. "He had kind of a British accent. He'd been educated at Oxford for a few years before returning to Syria. We had studied many of the same subjects so we had a lot in common." She bit her bottom lip. "When we didn't want anyone else to understand our conversation, we'd speak in English."

"You really liked this guy, didn't you?" Isaac seemed to understand.

"No. I thought I loved him." She grimaced, then admitted, "He was just using me to get the locations of our next raids. The women's battalion concentrated on finding and freeing children who had been kidnapped by ISIS."

She shook her head and looked out the kitchen window. "I was such an idiot. I don't know why I never saw it. So many times our teams would arrive hours too late. The girls had already been moved." Withholding the anger and controlling her voice, she told Isaac, "All those times, if I had kept my mouth shut, we could have saved those girls."

She grabbed the bottle of water and tried to wash away the lump stuck in her throat. "He betrayed me." She could hear the vehemence in those three simple words but tamped down the hatred in order to explain. "I trusted him with the lives of those girls and the women I fought next to. There were several occasions when one of my soldiers was wounded or killed in a raid. When I discovered what he'd done...I couldn't let him do it again."

With no inflection in his voice, Isaac asked, "So you killed him?"

"No, damn it." Then she reconsidered. He was dead due to her actions. "I didn't pull the trigger, but once I found out who he really was, I turned him in."

"So, he's still alive?"

"No. He died while trying to escape." She would never forget the pain in her heart when the colonel had told her about his death. Part of her had been elated that she didn't have to worry about him finding out that she'd been the one to turn him in. She had seen Aziz's temper on more than one occasion, although he'd never focused that anger on her. She'd never imagined that his brother would order his followers to come after her, especially in the USA.

"How did you find out he wasn't who he said he was?"

"My visa was about to expire, and I really missed my parents. I wanted to go home and see them." Hannah swallowed hard. "I wanted to surprise Aziz and get him a visa to come to the United States with me. I thought, like the young fool I was, that our relationship was moving on to the next step. We had even talked about children, although he had never asked me to marry him. I wanted my mom and dad to meet him."

Isaac simply nodded. "Go on."

"I was at the U.S. Embassy and had just gotten my visa renewed so I could come back to Syria after going home. I gave the clerk Aziz's name. A few minutes later, she spun the screen around so I could see his picture and confirm it was him. Not only was he on the no-fly list, but it also said he was the only brother of Abu Bakr al-Baghdadi."

"The head of ISIS?" Isaac confirmed.

All Hannah could do was nod her head.

"You were sleeping with the Caliphate's brother," he accused.

"I didn't know that at the time," she threw back at him. "Look, I was young and stupid. I had dated in college, but all of a sudden I'm halfway around the world in the middle of a war zone and this handsome, intelligent, older man who speaks my native language starts paying attention to me." She threw her hands up and let them fall back into her lap. "No one knew who he was, least of all me."

"And because you turned in his brother who got killed during his arrest, al-Baghdadi wants you dead." Isaac had summed it up quickly.

"Yes." Tears streamed down her face. "I really fucked things up. I went to Syria to help the kidnapped girls. Sure, we were able to save a few hundred, but my naïveté and big mouth kept hundreds more in slavery. And the things those men do to those little girls makes me sick."

She was crying so hard she could hardly catch her breath. "I don't give a shit about their civil war. The Sunnis and Kurds have been fighting for hundreds of years. I wish they would kill each other off completely. I just don't want them harming young girls ever again."

Isaac came around the table. He picked her up out of the chair and carried her to the living room where he sat in one of the rocker recliners, placing her across his lap. "It'll be okay, sweetheart. You're safe here with me."

He knew the truth, yet was still willing to comfort her, protect her.

In that moment, safe in his arms, she knew what love really was…acceptance of her, flaws and all.

Isaac kissed her forehead and then tucked her head under his chin.

In that instant, Hannah fell a little in love with Isaac.

CHAPTER 11

"Snowman checking in. Any news?"

Karl was back on the operations center desk that morning. It had been four days since Isaac had passed Hannah's information up the chain of command. They'd had four days of honeymoon-like bliss.

Their days were filled with checking the perimeter, finding only fox, moose, and elk tracks in the freshly fallen snow within one mile of the cabin. Mealtimes had become extremely domestic. He always cooked breakfast since discovering Hannah was not a morning person, but that could've been his fault. His insatiable morning hard-on meant at least an hour of lovemaking and multiple orgasms for Hannah before he'd take his own release. He'd then sneak out of bed to allow her to sleep again.

Several times, day and night, Hannah had reached for him, or he for her. They had christened nearly every flat surface in the cabin, but the soft rug in front of the burning fireplace had become their favorite. He loved that she was such an adventurous lover, willing to try new things. She'd even suggested several.

"Good news, my friend, you're headed back to Atlanta." Karl's statement shocked Isaac out of his fantasy world.

"What do you mean?" Isaac looked down the hallway to where the woman he realized he'd been falling in love with lay amidst rumpled sheets. He didn't want to leave the insulated world they had created. He didn't want to lose her.

"Al-Baghdadi is dead. USSOCOM sent in a SpecOps team six hours ago. We have DNA confirmation. With his brother gone, thanks to your little sweetie, the entire organization is in upheaval." Karl then added in a casual tone, "I found the greatest bar in the Buckhorn District. These women are off the charts beautiful and looking for nothing more than a good time."

Isaac couldn't imagine sleeping with any other woman now that he'd had Hannah. Even the thought felt like infidelity.

"How soon do you think you can get her down the mountain into Bozeman?"

They were supposed to leave now? No. He needed more time with Hannah. He didn't want this to end. Sometime in the last week, he had fallen in love with the most interesting, gorgeous, wonderful woman with the biggest heart he'd ever known.

Maybe he could delay at least another day. Neither had dared think about the future with ISIS so hot on their tails. But, now, their possibilities were wide open. They would return to Atlanta together. She could move in with him, just to be sure this thing they had worked in the real world.

"Hey, Snowman, you still with me?" Karl's voice broke into his thoughts.

"Yeah, I'm here." With this mindset, Isaac told his best friend, "It'll take us at least forty-eight hours to work our way to Bozeman."

"Work faster," Karl insisted. "Alex already has a jet headed your way. It seems Homeland Security wants to talk with Ms. Kader."

Well, damn. He had no choice but to go wake up Hannah. It would take at least an hour to close down the cabin and another few hours to ski down to the main road. The wet snow and warmer temperatures they'd gotten over the past two days would make the going slow.

"Give me four hours and send a vehicle toward Ennis on State Route 287." Isaac hated the fact they had to leave immediately, but now he and Hannah could have a future together. "I'll ping our location when we reach the highway."

"Let me know when you switch to field communications. In the meantime, call if anything changes. Atlanta Center out." The line went dead.

Phone still in his hand, Isaac walked to his bedroom. Standing in the doorway, he stared at Hannah. In sleep, she looked so peaceful. Now she could wear that expression all the time. The threat to her life was gone.

Unfortunately, they were now on a timetable.

He sat on the edge of the big bed and ran his fingers through her silky brown hair. "Hannah, sweetheart, you need to wake up. I have good news." He bent over and kissed her, wanting to crawl back into the bed and take her one more time...but he couldn't.

He smiled at the thought that the next time they made love, it would be in his bed in Atlanta. Hurrying toward that mental picture, he brushed the hair from her face and watched her awaken.

An hour later, clean sheets folded back in the linen closet, every dish scrubbed and placed in cabinets, Isaac walked through the cabin that would forever hold so many special memories. Once he was back home, he would have to call his uncle Samuel and thank him for the use of the secluded home. Given that he was still in work mode, he couldn't take the time to thank the man in person.

All power off, Isaac reset the battery-operated house alarm system and closed the keys inside the secret log panel. He turned to find Hannah strapping on her skis.

"As soon as you have your gear on, switch on your earpiece." Isaac tapped the button and then screwed his small communication unit into his ear.

Before he had a chance to confirm his connection with Atlanta Center, three men in winter camouflage stepped from behind large pine trees with mini submachine guns pointed at him. His pistol was at the small of his back, but he'd be dead before he could even reach it.

One of the men boldly stepped out from behind a one-hundred-year-old tree and lifted his heat-shielding balaclava. Probably their entire suit was shielding their body temperature from the thermal satellite. It was no wonder the Atlanta ops center hadn't detected them.

"Hannah, it's time for you to come home and be with your husband." The man's gun was directly pointed at her.

Her jaw dropped and her eyes grew huge. "Aziz?".

"Yes, my dear." He chuckled. "You didn't really think I was dead, did you?"

"But...but the colonel told me you were shot while trying to escape arrest." Hannah's face passed from confusion to anger and finally calculation.

"You can't believe everything you hear." A slash of white showed between his nearly black mustache and long beard. "Especially when it comes from a faithful follower of Al-Baghdadi. Part of what the colonel told you was true, I did escape...with his help." Mockingly, Aziz asked, "Did you mourn for me?" He stared at her for a moment. "You did." His smile was not one of pleasure but of satisfaction. "Good. I prefer my wives to love me."

Anger flashed in her huge brown eyes. "I am not your wife."

"The ceremony is only a formality. I claimed you over a year ago." His gaze swept over her helmet, down her ski jacket to the snow pants. He shook his head. "You will need to learn to set aside Western ways. No man is allowed to look at my wives. It's a good thing I brought you an abaya and niqab." His gaze swept the area. "I will allow you to ski off this mountain in those clothes, but you will change into appropriate clothing before my men pick us up. We need to return to Iraq so I can properly bury my brother and take his place as Caliphate."

Isaac watched in horror as the future leader of ISIS planned to kidnap the woman he loved.

Hannah shook her head. "That's not going to happen. I'm not going anywhere with you, certainly not to Iraq. And you may think you have some claim on me, but you have none. I could never marry a man like you. My biggest regret in life was ever falling in love with you and, yes, I thought I loved you." She looked directly at Isaac. "That was before I knew what real love was."

Did that mean Hannah loved him? Isaac's heart swelled.

"Snowman, Atlanta Center, what the hell is going on?" Karl's voice sounded controlled, but concerned, in his ear. "Do you have company?"

Isaac didn't dare speak. Although he had guns pointed at him, he certainly didn't want to draw any more attention to himself than necessary.

"Blow once for yes, twice for no," Karl ordered.

Through tight lips, Isaac expelled one burst of air.

Hannah's hands were still in her pockets, and he saw the move. He needed to be ready for anything. They would take out the enemy and escape down the mountain.

Aziz slowly moved his head from side to side. "Oh, my sweet, innocent Hannah. You don't under-stand. I will give you a choice, come back to Iraq with me. You see, with you as my wife, you can help me unite Syria and Iraq. Eventually, the land all the way through Afghanistan will be in my control. No one over there needs to know about your American citi-zenship. That will be our dirty little secret, but one we will use to get arms and billions of dollars in support from the United States to help establish my new government. Your politicians can all take credit for bringing peace to the Middle East, but we will both know it was you."

Oh, fuck. Would she take the bait? Aziz would use

her as a pawn in his game for power and domination while beating her bright spirit into submission.

But Isaac was not going to let her go without a fight. Very slowly, he moved his hand toward the small of his back where he'd tucked a .45 caliber pistol.

"Snowman, how many tangos?" Isaac was glad Atlanta Center was on board. He released three short bursts.

"And what's my other choice?" Hannah's voice was surprisingly steady. At least she hadn't jumped on his first suggestion.

Aziz shrugged. "I kill you now."

Bam. Bam.

"Not if I kill you first." Hannah had shot Aziz in the thigh, very close to his manhood.

A second man crumpled to the ground.

Isaac had whipped out his gun and shot the other two men. One bullet went through the man's helmet, and Isaac caught the second man in the shoulder as he fell to the ground.

"Go," Isaac screamed to Hannah. She was ready to move but he didn't even have on his skis.

"I hear gunshots," Karl announced in his ear. "What's going on?"

"Too busy to talk," Isaac replied.

Hannah used her pole to knock Aziz's gun out of his hand then dug both poles into the snow. She shoved off down the mountain, zigzagging through trees.

Smart woman. They had no idea if Aziz had backup or a sniper hiding in the trees.

Isaac shot both men in the neck. They were down and not ever going to move again.

Running, he grabbed his skis and threw them on the ground, stepping into the bindings as he slid on his backpack. When they had practiced this in Alaska as SEALs, he never imagined he'd be running from the enemy on his home turf.

He took one last look at Aziz as his blood turned the pristine snow a deep red. His gun was ten feet away. Isaac considered for a moment leaving him so he could bleed out slowly. He would remain conscious for several minutes knowing he was going to die. The final torture seemed appropriate for everything he knew about the man.

Instead, Isaac put a bullet in his heart.

Isaac didn't bother checking for a pulse. He had to get to Hannah. She could ski like the wind. They had to cross an open snowfield where they would both be vulnerable, and he wanted to be there to protect her in case there were other tangos nearby.

"Three dead at the cabin including al-Habib," Isaac reported to Atlanta Center. "I'm trying to catch up to Hannah now. We're back on Plan A."

"Roger that," Karl acknowledged.

Bending his knees and tucking in, Isaac chose the

straightest path possible through the dense forest. Keeping her ski trail in sight, Isaac emerged from the woods and immediately stopped. He scanned for the double line in the snow.

She had vanished as though into thin air.

"Isaac." Hannah's voice was filled with relief as she stepped out of the shadows and skied toward him. He had never seen anything more beautiful in his life. She didn't stop until she ran into his body, her skis sliding perfectly between his.

She threw her arms around his neck and pulled him close. "Thank God. I was so worried. I heard several more shots."

"They're all dead," he reassured her. "Now let's get the hell off this mountain and back to Atlanta." He kissed her hard one more time. The words *I love you* were right there on his tongue. They just wouldn't come out. "I know that wasn't easy to shoot Aziz."

She smiled back at him. "Yes, it was. But I guess I'm better at long-distance shots than I am up close. I wanted to shoot his dick off." She walked her skis backward then turned her tips down the wide-open slope.

Isaac could do nothing but follow her in wonderment. He already knew he was in love with her, but he had just fallen a little deeper.

They were more than halfway down the half-mile-wide swath of deep snow when the crack of a rifle shot broke through their peaceful trek. Isaac looked over his shoulder to see Aziz three hundred feet down the slope from the tree line, a sniper rifle at his shoulder. He had something tied around his upper thigh.

Isaac cursed himself for not checking for a pulse. In retrospect, of course the man was probably wearing body armor. The direct shot to his chest no doubt broke a few ribs, but obviously hadn't killed him.

Hannah had already folded her body into a tuck and pointed her skis straight downhill.

The sound of a second shot bounced off the trees.

The earth beneath Isaac shook.

Avalanche.

Isaac immediately looked for Hannah. She had already kicked off her skis and her vest was inflating. He looked up the mountain to see the snow crack a hundred feet above Aziz.

Good. He had caused this avalanche and hopefully, it would kill him.

Isaac reached to pull the cord for his own airbag when he was hit by a wall of snow. Training took over, and he slammed his hand to activate his location transponder.

Cold. That was the first thing Isaac realized as he came to. He thought he heard his name, but it was so faint. He pushed his hands up toward his face to dig out space to breathe as he'd been taught in avalanche school. He had no idea which way was up or down.

He wondered, obviously too late, if activating his airbag would give him more space.

"Isaac. Can you hear me?"

This time he was sure he'd heard Hannah's voice.

Creating an air pocket in front of his face, he called out, "Hannah, I'm here."

Snow moved around him. When he tried to kick to give more room for his legs, pain shot all the way through his body. He wiggled his toes. Thank God they worked. When he tried to move his ankles, the pain was so great he almost passed out.

Weight lifted above his belly as light filtered through. He was obviously lying on his back. He punched through the snow and waved his hands.

"Oh, thank God!" Hannah was digging with her hands and removed the snow in front of his face. "Are you all right?"

"I am now." He shifted and cried out in pain. "My leg."

It took fifteen minutes for Hannah to remove enough snow to pull him out. Every time he shifted, he fought back the blackness that threatened to close down his mind.

"Take my wrists," she ordered.

Bracing himself against the pain he knew would come, she managed to drag him to the surface.

While digging him out, she had been talking with Karl at the Atlanta Operations Center through the communication unit in her ear. A local search and rescue team had already been dispatched and was on their way to evacuate him.

Another team, this one from Homeland Security, stealthily headed toward the cabin. Only a few people would ever know of the carnage that had happened there.

Thankful to see the sun again, Isaac dragged in a deep breath. When he lifted his head to look at his leg, he almost passed out. He recognized he had a concussion.

Hannah's face filled his view when he opened his eyes. "I was so worried I wouldn't get to you in time." Surrounded by snow and unconscious, the body could freeze within twenty minutes. Simply breathing was another way to die in an avalanche— from carbon dioxide poisoning.

She then bent and touched his cold lips with hers. His whole body warmed from his heart outward. She was his, and he wanted to make sure she knew it, but he was fast falling off the adrenaline high. Darkness was encroaching the edges of his mind. He had to say the words, now.

"I love you." The last thing he saw before he passed out was her beautiful smile.

"I love you, too." Hannah's words carried him into blissful darkness.

EPILOGUE

"Well, you're looking better today," Pete said as he stepped into Isaac's hospital room, Mark right behind him. They set a white paper bag and foam cups on the tray. "You couldn't leave Montana without having a buffalo burger."

Hannah smiled and chided, "You'd better have brought one of those for me, too." She released Isaac's hand and dug into the bag.

Pete slung an arm around her shoulders. "I would never forget you." He looked at Isaac. "You have yourself one special little lady here."

"That I do," he admitted. Except for during surgery, she had never left his side. She'd been there through the helicopter ride to the hospital and every minute since he left the recovery room.

She laid out their meal and dug in.

"So, you ever going to tell us why there are at least

130

half a dozen big black SUVs running around the area?" Pete asked for what had to be the fifth time. "You can't turn around in Big Sky without bumping into feds in suits and sunglasses."

Isaac shrugged. "I've been sworn to secrecy."

"So, how exactly are you going to get home?" Mark asked, changing the subject. "I hope they will at least put you in first-class so you can stretch out that leg. You are damn lucky the bullet only went through the muscle."

Isaac chuckled. "Tell me that when I start rehab next week."

He couldn't see who walked through the door, but instantly knew who it was when Alex spoke. "You ready to get out of here?"

Isaac felt the need to sit up straighter in his boss's presence. "Yes, sir."

Alex slapped him on the shoulder then leaned in to sniff the burgers. "You think we can get some of those to go? They don't look like any hospital food I've ever seen."

"They're buffalo burgers," Hannah explained and held out her hand. "Hannah Kader. Nice to meet you." She set the burger down and then threw her arms around Alex. "I can't thank you enough for everything you guys did for me."

Awkwardly, Alex patted her on the back. "That's what we do." When he turned, Isaac noticed the gorgeous blonde. "I'd like you to meet my fiancée,

131

Katlin Callahan."

With confidence, the woman strode to Hannah and shook her hand. "We need to talk, but unfortunately, I'm the one flying the plane back to Atlanta, so it'll have to wait until I get the two of you home safe."

"Isaac, I promised I'd introduce you to Guardian Security's other partner. Meet Katlin Callahan." When her stunning blue-on-blue eyes met his, he understood what Alex had said days ago about never underestimating a woman.

"It's a pleasure to meet you, ma'am."

She returned his firm shake. "I wanted to personally thank you both for disposing of one of the world's greatest threats. Al-Habib was more dangerous than his brother." Katlin spoke as though she had personal knowledge of the facts. For some reason, Isaac didn't doubt it.

Alex clapped his hands together. "Okay, let's see what we can do about getting you released." He then turned around and faced Pete and Mark. "I want to thank the two of you for being willing to back up my man. Had I known the way things were going to go down, I would've pulled you in from the beginning. Next time." He shook hands with both men and then disappeared through the door.

Pete stepped up beside the bed. "Well, it looks like we may get to work together sometime in the future. I hope, though, we'll get to see you before then."

Isaac took Hannah's hand. "We'll see you at the

wedding this summer. Hannah and I have decided to get married here in Big Sky."

Mark burst out laughing. "Usually people honeymoon here, not get married."

"Oh, we're going to do both," Hannah informed the room. She squeezed Isaac's hand. "There's this wonderful little cabin that already holds some very special memories."

Pete slapped Mark on the shoulder. "We need to hit the road and get back to our wives. Be sure to send us invitations."

"Of course." Hannah and Isaac had spoken at the same time. They looked at each other and smiled. They were already one soul.

The End

MORE BOOKS BY KALYN COOPER

Black Swan Series

MILITARY ACTIVE DUTY WOMEN SECRETLY TRAINED IN Special Operations and the men who dare to capture the heart of a Woman Warrior.

Unconventional Beginnings Prequel (Black Swan novella #0.5) ~ He's dead. But they can't allow it to affect her. She's too important.
Download FREE
https://dl.bookfunnel.com/uec4utb66d

Unrelenting Love: Lady Hawk (Katlin) & Alex (Black Swan novel #1) ~ Women in special operations? Never… Until he sleeps with the most lethal woman in the world.

Noel's Puppy Power: Bailey & Tanner (A Sweet Christmas Black Swan novella #1.5) ~ He's better at communicating with animals than women, but as an amputee she knows firsthand it's the internal scars that can be most difficult to heal.

Uncaged Love: Harper & Rafe (Black Swan novel #2) ~ The jungle isn't the only thing that's hot while escaping from a Colombian cartel.

Unexpected Love: Lady Eagle (Grace) & Griffin (Black Swan novel #3) ~ He never believed in love, but he never expected to find her.

Challenging Love: Katlin & Alex (A Black Swan novella #3.5) ~ A new relationship can be fragile when outsiders are determined to challenge that love.

Unguarded Love: Lady Harrier (Nita) & Daniel (Black Swan novel #4) ~ She couldn't lose another sick baby…then he brought her his dying daughter.

Choosing Love: Grace & Griffin (A Black Swan novella #4.5) ~ Hard choices have to be made when parents interfere in a growing relationship.

Unbeatable Love: Lady Falcon (Tori) & Marcus

(Black Swan novel #5) ~ Scarred outside and in, why would his beautiful friend ever want more with him?

Unmatched Love: Lady Kite (Lei Lu) & Henry
(Black Swan novel #6) ~ Scarred outside and in, why would his beautiful friend ever want more with him?

Unending Love: Lady Falcon (Tori) & Marcus
(Black Swan novel #7) ~ Their life together is not over. He has to believe it...or it will be.

Guardian ELITE Series

Former special operators, these men work for Guardian Security (from the Black Swan Series) protecting families in their homes and executives on the road, but they can't always protect their hearts.

ELITE Redemption (Guardian ELITE Book 1) ~ Guarding a billionaire and his wife isn't easy when you can't keep your eyes off your bikini wearing, gun carrying partner who is lethal in stilettos. *This book was previously published as **Double Jeopardy**.*

ELITE Justice (Guardian ELITE Book 2) ~ She's not what she seems. Neither is he. But the terrorist threat is real. So is the desire that smolders between

136

them. *This book was previously published as **Justice for Gwen.***

ELITE Rescue (Guardian ELITE Book 3) ~ When Jacin awoke stateside, he remembered nothing about his escape from the Colombian cartel or his torture. He was sure of only one thing, his love of Melina, his handler. When she disappears, neither bruises nor the CIA will keep him from rescuing her. *This book was previously published as Rescuing Melina.*

ELITE Protection (Guardian ELITE Book 4) ~ Terrorists want her...but so does he. The chase isn't the only thing that heats up when the flint of the former SEAL strikes against the steel of the woman warrior. *This book was previously published as Snow SEAL.*

ELITE Defense (Guardian ELITE Book 5) ~ Guarding her wasn't his job, but he couldn't let her die...even before she stole his heart. When he discovers the temptingly beautiful foreign service officer is being threatened, his protective instincts take over. *This book was previously published as Securing Willow.*

ELITE Damnit (Guardian ELITE Book 6) ~ With a hurricane bearing down on the tiny island, they only have days to find and rescue ten kidnapped young girls and their chaperones…and keep their hands off each other. *This book was previously published as a short story titled Damnit I Love You.*

Suspense Sisters

The Shadow SEALs were once the best of the best, recruited from obscurity after their fall from grace to work in the shadows, enacting justice upon our enemies and protecting those caught in the crosshairs by any means necessary.

Shadow in the Mountain Another mission into the shadows was the last place he wanted to be. Last time it ended his career. This time promises death or salvation.

Shadow in the Daylight After he left the SEALs, Andrew did a covert job for Charley before parting ways. As the Security Officer aboard a cruise ship, he invited several SEAL friends to travel as his guests through the Panama Canal. He never imagined he'd need their highly trained skills.

Cancun Series

ELITE PROTECTION

Follow the Girard family —along with their friends, former SEALs and active duty female Navy pilots—as they hunt Mayan antiquities, terrorists and Mexican cartels in what most would call paradise. Tropical nights aren't the only thing HOT in Cancun.

Christmas in Cancun (Cancun Series Book #1) ~ Can the former SEAL keep his libido in check and his family safe when the quest for ancient Mayan idols turns murderous?

Conquered in Cancun (Cancun Series Novella #1.5) ~ A helicopter pilot's second chance at love walks into a Cancun nightclub, but she's a jet fighter pilot with reinforced walls around her heart.

Captivated in Cancun (Cancun Series Book #2) ~ His job is tracking down terrorists so he's not interested in a family. She wants him short-term, then needs him when their worlds collide.

Claimed by a SEAL (Cancun Series crossover Novella #2.5 with Cat Johnson's Hot SEALs) ~ How far will the Homeland Security agent go to assure mission success when forced undercover for a second time with an irresistible SEAL?

139

Never Forgotten Trilogy

The mission brought the five of them together, disaster nearly tore them apart, a mystery and killer reunited them forever.

A Love Never Forgotten (Never Forgotten novel #1) ~ Dreams or nightmares. Truth or lies. He can't tell them apart. Then he discovers the woman who has haunted his dreams is real. Is she his future? Or his past?

A Promise Never Forgotten (Never Forgotten novel #2) ~ As a Marine Lieutenant Colonel, he could take on any mission and succeed. Raising his two godchildren...with her...just might kill him.

A Moment Never Forgotten (Never Forgotten novel #3) ~ The moment he realized she was in serious danger...he couldn't protect her.

ABOUT THE AUTHOR

KaLyn Cooper is a USA Today Bestselling author whose romances blend fact and fiction with blazing heat and heart-pounding suspense. Life as a military wife has shown KaLyn the world, and thirty years in PR taught her that fact can be stranger than fiction. She leaves it up to the reader to separate truth from imagination. She, her husband, and Little Bear (Alaskan Malamute) live in Tennessee on a micro-plantation filled with gardens, cattle, and quail. When she's not writing, she's at the shooting range or paddling on the river.

For the latest on works in progress and future releases, check out
   KaLyn Cooper's website www.KaLyn-Cooper.com

Follow **KaLyn Cooper on Facebook** for promotions and giveaways
   https://www.
facebook.com/KaLynCooper1Author/

Sign up for exclusive promotions and special offers only available in **KaLyn's newsletter** https://kalyncooper.com/kalyn-cooper-newsletter